SECOND CHANCE COLTON

Marie Ferrarella

D0032483

H HARLEQUIN®ROMANTIC SUSPENSE

Special thanks and acknowledgment are given to
Marie Ferrarella for her contribution
to the Coltons of Oklahoma miniseries.

ISBN-13: 978-0-373-27937-1

Second Chance Colton

Copyright © 2015 by Harlequin Books S.A.

Recycling programs for this product may not exist in your area.

Printed in U.S.A.

Praise for Marie Ferrarella

"Expert storytelling moves the book along at a steady pace. A solidly crafted plot makes it quite entertaining."
— *RT Book Reviews* on *Cavanaugh Fortune*

"A joy to read."
— *RT Book Reviews* on *Christmas Cowboy Duet*

"Heartwarming. That's the way I have described every book by Marie Ferrarella that I have read. *In the Family Way* engenders in me the same warm, fuzzy feeling that I have come to expect from her books."
— *The Romance Reader*

"Ms. Ferrarella warms our hearts with her charming characters and delicious interplay."
— *RT Book Reviews* on *A Husband Waiting to Happen*

"Ms. Ferrarella creates fiery, strong-willed characters, an intense conflict and an absorbing premise no reader could possibly resist."
— *RT Book Reviews* on *A Match for Morgan*

* * *

Be sure to check out the next books in The Coltons of Oklahoma miniseries.
The Coltons of Oklahoma: **Family secrets always find a way to resurface...**

If you're on Twitter, tell us what you think of Harlequin Romantic Suspense! #harlequinromsuspense

Dear Reader,

I have always been a firm believer in second chances—both in giving them and in getting them. You don't always get things right the first time around. The first time around, things are new, untried. Scary. The first time around, I failed my driving test (and the second time, and the third time, until I got a DMV tester under the age of fifty who wasn't afraid of dying—but I digress). I've been driving for thirty-six years now (I got my license at the age of three) and things have gone very well, thank you. The point is, you should never do things only once and if they don't go according to plan, just give up. You deserve a second chance, as does everyone else.

Ryan Colton certainly deserved a second chance to get things right after he broke up with the only woman he was destined to love. He was a marine at the time, going off to fight and not wanting the burden of knowing that his lady, Susie Howard, was back home, worrying about his safety. It was kinder (or so he thought) to let her move on with her life. Ten years later finds them having inadvertently "moved on" into each other's spheres. This is what second chances are for.

Thank you for taking the time to pick up my book and read it. And as always, from the bottom of my heart, I wish you someone to love who loves you back.

Best,

Marie

This *USA TODAY* bestselling and RITA® Award-winning author has written 250 books for Harlequin, some under the name Marie Nicole. Her romances are beloved by fans worldwide. Visit her website, marieferrarella.com.

Books by Marie Ferrarella

Harlequin Romantic Suspense

The Adair Affairs

Carrying His Secret

Cavanaugh Justice

The Cavanaugh Code
In Bed with the Badge
Cavanaugh Judgment
Cavanaugh Reunion
A Cavanaugh Christmas
Cavanaugh's Bodyguard
Cavanaugh Rules
Cavanaugh's Surrender
Cavanaugh on Duty
Mission: Cavanaugh Baby
Cavanaugh Hero
Cavanaugh Undercover
Cavanaugh Strong
Cavanaugh Fortune

Visit the Author Profile page at Harlequin.com for more titles.

To
Carly Silver,
and
Brave New Frontiers

Prologue

There was a time when he loved coming up to this ranch. Loved riding through its fields, getting lost in its acreage.

Right now, that time seemed as if it were a million years ago. Back then he'd been a boy and this had been his ranch.

Well, his and his family's, Ryan Colton amended silently.

Back then, the only crimes, large or small, harmless or serious, had all been made-up, part of the make-believe games he, his brothers Jack, Eric and Brett, as well as his half brother, Daniel, and his baby sister, Greta, would play.

Playing had been serious business back then.

He wished for a moment that he could go back to that point in time. Back to when innocence had been a major player in all their lives.

But a lot of things had happened since then. Jack had gotten married, become a father and then gotten divorced before he finally got it right and found Tracy. Eric had left the ranch to become a trauma surgeon at Tulsa General Hospital, where he had met Kara, the love of his life. Daniel, along with his wife Megan, and Brett and his wife, Hannah, were still here on the ranch, along with Jack, but Daniel and Brett had ideas about managing the ranch that differed from the direction that Jack had initially wanted to take. All three were currently trying to iron things out rather than clashing over methods the way they had once done.

And Greta, well, Greta was Greta. Her gift for training horses took her away from the ranch a great deal more than it once had. These days found her in Oklahoma City more than here because of her engagement to Mark Stanton. But even when she was gone, her presence seemed to just ooze out of the very shadows, as if unconsciously reminding the others that she, too, was a Colton and every bit as much a part of this ranch as they were.

As for him, well, he had gone into the Marines in search of himself. He came back still looking, except now he did it as a homicide detective with the Tulsa police department.

And it was in that capacity, as a police detective rather than a Colton sibling, that he was here now, standing in one of the Lucky C's smaller stables, staring at a broken windowpane with blood smeared on the jagged edges.

Whose blood was it and why had they broken in? Other than defacing some of the property, he saw no reason for this. Nothing seemed to have been taken.

But it was obvious that something sinister was going on here at the Lucky C—something that seemed to call the ranch's very name into question.

This wasn't the first time he'd been called up to the ranch to investigate a sinister occurrence. In the past few months there had been a series of "mishaps," for lack of a better word, Ryan thought darkly as he methodically examined the crime scene.

There'd been the fire that'd started up for no apparent reason—no faulty wiring, no carelessly discarded matches or cigarette butts—and several wanton, senseless acts of vandalism. And there was that break-in that had occurred just the other day, also with no particular rhyme or reason to it.

And then there had been that initial break-in at the main house, shortly after Greta's engagement party, that had been the start of it all. Someone had broken in and stolen some things—and beaten his mother in the process. Beaten her senseless. Jack had been the one to find her that day. Ryan didn't want to think about what the possible consequences of that beating could have been if he hadn't.

As it was, Abra Colton had remained in the hospital for some time, in a coma and all but lost to all of them. He'd thought his father would come completely apart during that time.

Mercifully, his mother was out of the hospital now and back home, but when he'd finally questioned her, she'd been unable to shed any real light on what had happened to provoke that attack—or, more important, the name of the person who had attacked her. Her testimony—when his mother was finally up to giving it—had been jumbled and vague.

And then she had just shut down, saying she didn't want to "speak of it." Afraid for her mental state, Ryan knew better than to try to push her. So he was resigned to waiting until such time as his mother was ready to "speak of it."

He sighed, moving slowly about this latest crime scene. His mother's attack—and the robbery—had been the beginning. These other senseless acts of destruction had followed, but they'd left no discernible pattern.

What he was now looking at was the most recent of several lesser acts of vandalism that had befallen the family. The Lucky C, it seemed, had found itself at the very center of some strange activity—activity that just reeked of malice.

The only thing Ryan knew with certainty was

that the attack, the acts that had followed, weren't random, the way he'd initially hoped. Someone definitely had it in for his family.

The questions that were on the table now were why and who?

He knew that he was too close to this. But who had more of an incentive to solve this thing than he did? Whoever had orchestrated this had already tried—unsuccessfully, thank God—to eliminate his mother, Abra, from the family tree. He didn't want to hang back, spinning theories and coming up empty, potentially leaving the ranch and his family wide-open for another all-out assault.

Who knew, the next time it might not just be a broken window he'd find himself dealing with, but someone's broken neck.

This had to stop before then.

Ryan frowned. He needed to put the call in for the crime scene unit to get out here. They had a sharper eye for this sort of thing than he did. With luck and their combined efforts, he could put an end to this, whatever "this" was.

With luck.

The very phrase mocked him, but he was determined to get to the bottom of all this.

And soon.

He *had* to.

Chapter 1

"You're wrong."

Ryan Colton's booming, resonant voice filled every available nook and cranny within the small, albeit state-of-the-art, Tulsa PD forensic lab.

"No, I'm not."

Susie Howard, the lab's chief forensic expert, refused to be intimidated and stood her ground, even though a part of her could understand why the homicide detective before her had balked. After all, she'd just told him that the person who had broken into and apparently vandalized one of the ranch's stables—and was possibly responsible for the numerous vandalisms that had occurred prior to this latest one—was his sister, Greta.

But like it or not, Susie thought, evidence was evidence.

Doing her best to sound professional and remain removed—no easy feat in this case—Susie stated the obvious. "You asked me to put a rush on the DNA evidence, so I did. The sample from the Lucky C's crime scene went to the head of the line and that's your answer," she told him, tapping the name that had been generated by her trusty machine after the test had been completed. Greta Colton's prints and DNA were in the system because of the nature of her work.

Frowning, Susie withdrew her well-manicured finger. "I can't help it if you don't like the answer, but that's it. The machine doesn't lie—even if you think that I do," she concluded, her hazel eyes narrowing as she tossed her head. A blond tendril came loose from the tightly wound bun she wore at the back of her neck as she looked up at the six-foot-two detective.

Ryan struggled to keep his temper in check. It had grown very frayed lately. Yelling wasn't going to get him anywhere, he knew that. Especially not with Susie.

But she just couldn't be right.

She *couldn't* be.

His words were carefully measured as he spoke. "I didn't say you were lying, but there's always the possibility that there's a margin of error."

Which was what he was pinning all his hopes

on now. He *knew* Greta, had watched her grow up. There was no reason he could come up with for why she would do something like this.

"Run the test again," Ryan instructed, his voice leaving no room for argument. "I don't want to tell you your job—"

"Then don't!" Susie retorted.

Ryan continued on the subject as if she hadn't said a single word. "But there was enough blood on that broken window to take several swabs. Run a second sample. And a third if you need to," he added before the forensic expert could protest.

"How many do you want me to run before you accept the results?" Susie challenged.

"Just run the test again," Ryan ordered, doing his best to remain removed from the discussion.

Fat chance of that. The woman who had just told him that the blood belonged to his sister, Greta, was the same woman he had once been seriously involved with. The same woman, after their relationship had become serious, he had deliberately cut off all ties with.

He'd been a Marine back then, home on leave, when their paths had first crossed. They had hit it off instantly—hot and heavy, and very, very serious. He spent every moment he could with her, and she with him. Neither of their families knew about their relationship because they never made time for anyone else. It was as if somehow, subconsciously, they both understood that they were on a timetable. When he received word that he was being deployed overseas again, Susie had naturally been upset, but she'd promised to wait for him no matter how long it took.

That had been the problem. The burden of having someone waiting for him, loving him and praying for his safe return, was just too much for him to carry into battle. The weight of that responsibility threatened to sap away his edge, to blur his focus, and survival depended heavily on focus.

Besides, if he didn't make it back, he knew how that could affect the rest of Susie's life—how it could *destroy* the rest of her life. He couldn't do anything about the way his family reacted to news like that, but he could do something about Susie.

There was far too much guilt attached to their relationship for him, so he chose the simple way out. He broke things off between them—doing so in a letter rather than in person.

In effect, he had chosen the coward's way out. He never found out how she felt about the breakup because Susie never wrote back. Eventually, he convinced himself that that was for the best and that this was the way things were meant to be. He was meant to be alone.

With that in mind, he struggled to move on, to move forward. After his honorable discharge, he wound up becoming a police detective. In the beginning, it all boiled down to a matter of putting one foot in front of the other. And somehow, while he wasn't looking, six years managed to pass by.

He'd assumed he would never see Susie again. It got a little easier dealing with that with each year that went by.

The sight of Susie walking down the hall at the Tulsa police department one morning four years ago had completely knocked the air right out of him. But after a few seconds, he'd recovered and managed to push on.

For the past four years, they had politely but determinedly ignored one another, pretending not to be aware of the other person's existence whenever they found themselves in the same general vicinity. His cases were such that he found he didn't need any help from the forensic department.

But now, with the vandalism at the Lucky C amped up to a dangerous degree, Ryan resigned himself to the fact that he needed her help. Needed her training and her lab to help him solve this all-too-personal case he had taken on before things went from bad to fatal.

And now the attractive blonde who still sometimes turned up in his dreams had given him an answer that had all but left him numb and speechless. Was this her way of getting even with him for breaking up with her?

No, whatever else he might feel about Susie Howard, he knew that she had a great deal of integrity.

He was allowing his imagination to run away with him, something that didn't happen very often. He would be the first to admit that the situation had made him desperate.

He forced himself to remember that Susie wasn't the kind of person who would let her feelings get in the way of her work—and she certainly wasn't the type to frame an innocent person, no matter how much she might want to because she was in effect jilted by that person's older brother.

That wasn't the way Susie operated. Her sense of honor was something that he'd found admirable about her all those years ago.

Since he knew that Susie wasn't responsible for the results that were damning his sister, that left Ryan clinging to the only possible excuse he had left—that somehow, the periodically calibrated forensic equipment had malfunctioned.

Susie looked as if she was going to continue staunchly refusing to rerun the test. He had to get her to reverse that position.

"Do it for me," he requested, his voice as devoid of emotion as he could possibly render it. "Run the test again."

"Oh, well, if it's for you, sure, I'll run it again." There was more than a touch of sarcasm in Susie's voice. "And if it *wasn't* for you, I'd still run the test again, just because there seems to be some sort of doubt involved here," she went on to add icily. "I can see why finding out that your sister vandalized the family stables might be upsetting to you, so yes, I'll run the test again," she informed him coldly. "Now, if you don't mind getting out of my lab, I'll get started on that second test."

She turned her back on him, pretending that he was already gone.

She knew he wasn't because she could see his distorted reflection on the surface of her mass spectrometer. The machine was facing her. Her parting words to Ryan were "I'll have someone call you with the results once they're in."

When Ryan's reflection continued to remain exactly where it was, she asked in as disinterested a voice as she could summon, "Is there anything else?"

This had to be said. He knew that. If the air wasn't cleared between them, then she might be sorely tempted not to do her best job. He felt confident she wouldn't manufacture evidence, but he wasn't so sure that she'd bring her A game to the case.

"Yes," he said after a long moment, addressing the words to the back of Susie's head since she wasn't turning around again, "there's something else. I want to apologize for treating you so badly when I broke it off between us. But I did it for you, for your own good."

She almost swung around then, almost fired at him with both barrels, calling him an idiot and a fool—and a liar. Calling him an egotist for using that pathetic excuse when the real reason he had pulled his emotional vanishing act on her was because he'd obviously been afraid of commitment.

Any first-year psychology student would have been able to tell him that.

But she didn't swing around, didn't give Ryan a tongue-lashing and didn't tell him exactly what she thought. What would be the point? He had his lie, which he was holding on to for dear life, and she had moved on.

Or told herself she had.

So she remained facing her workbench, acting as if Ryan hadn't said a single word to her about their past or its abrupt ending.

"I'll have someone call you the minute the second results are in," she repeated.

This time, she saw his reflection retreat and then disappear.

Heard the door to the lab close again.

Only then did she turn around on her stool. "You jerk," Susie murmured, staring at the closed door. Her voice grew louder, more heated with every word she uttered. "You big, self-centered, blind, stupid, stupid jerk."

"Two degrees, six years in college and that's the best you can come up with?" Harold Gould marveled as the tall, thin lab assistant stepped out from the computer tech area where he had been working.

His white lab coat hung like a bland curtain about

his all but emaciated frame, giving the impression that it would begin flapping wildly about that same frame at the first sign of a breeze.

Startled, Susie's eyes met those of her junior assistant, who was also a lab intern. The brown eyes continued looking back at her, the assistant never flinching.

"I didn't know anyone else was here," Susie told the intern.

"Obviously. When I saw him walk in I was going to clear my throat in case something private was going to be said. But Colton started talking right away and it sounded kind of personal from the get-go." The look he gave her was sympathetic. "I didn't want to embarrass you."

"You just wanted to eavesdrop, hoping to score some juicy gossip," Susie countered.

She knew how the man operated. Harold Gould knew more about what was going on in the precinct after being here for a little more than three months than some of the twenty-year veterans did. It wasn't only lab procedures that he absorbed faster than a sponge.

The painfully thin shoulders rose and fell quickly, indicating that Harold had no intention of even attempting to contest her take on the situation. They both knew he enjoyed being a font of information, both technical and private.

"Yeah, well, there's that, too," he agreed, and then

he tried to set her mind at ease. "Don't worry, I don't have any time to talk to anyone so this isn't going into the rumor mill. And besides, I might be had for a song when it comes to certain things, but don't ever doubt my loyalty."

She liked Harold and was fairly certain that his heart was in the right place. But she'd paid the price for blind faith before and that had made her leery. Harold could just be offering her pretty words to distract her, Susie thought. "If it does hit the rumor mill, I'll know who to come after."

A small, amused smile played across all but non-existent lips. "Should I be shaking in my shoes now—or wait until later?" he asked her.

"Later," she told him. "We have work to do now." She glanced again at the closed door. "I'm going to have *you* run the DNA test on the blood this time."

"Really run the test, or...?" He raised one eyebrow, leaving the rest of the sentence unspoken but definitely understood.

Susie wanted to make one thing perfectly clear even as she cut the intern some slack because he was, after all, still relatively new.

"We don't do 'or' here, Harold. We don't even *think* about 'or.' Just one tiny instance—or even the *hint* of that kind of impropriety—and everything we've ever done here is going to be viewed as suspect and called into question. The amount of work that would be generated by something like that would be astronomical. Have I made that clear enough for you?"

She didn't want to come off as sounding belligerent, but there should be no question about how procedures were conducted.

"Just kidding, boss lady," Harold told her, raising his hands as a sign of surrender.

"I know. But it doesn't hurt to reiterate how we do things out loud every so often so that we don't *ever* lose sight of our function here. Because it only has to happen *once* and suddenly, we'll get our walking papers and be out on the street."

"Understood," Harold assured her. "But even so, you could stand to improve your vocabulary," he told her. "I could work up a whole host of multiple-syllable expletives you could hurl at yon studly homicide detective the next time your paths cross. You don't want to be caught unarmed, do you? Or worse, tongue-tied?" he concluded, pretending to shiver at the very thought of that happening.

"You miss the salient point. I don't want our paths crossing, *period*," she said, getting to the heart of the matter.

"For that even to be a remote possibility at this police precinct, one of you is going to have to put in for a transfer. Like, to a different city." Harold's shallow complexion seemed to brighten instantly as he thought over possibilities. "Do I get a vote as to which one of you should go?"

She wasn't about to feed the intern any more straight lines. Given half a chance, the man could go on talking for hours, like a windup toy whose spring had somehow malfunctioned and while she liked him and felt he did have a great deal of potential, she definitely didn't want to encourage him, especially not when there was work to do.

"Just do the test, Harold," Susie requested.

The lab intern saluted her comically as he said, "I hear and obey, my liege."

Susie rolled her eyes as she got back to her work.

Susie couldn't be right, Ryan stubbornly thought as he got back into his car. Starting it up, he pulled out of his parking spot, turned the sedan around and headed back to the Lucky C.

The forensic team, obviously, had come and gone. They had a reputation for being very thorough. Although he had been the one to initially call them in to see if he had missed something, he wanted to go back and go over the latest crime scene one more time to see if perhaps *they* had missed something this time around.

It was worth a shot. What did he have to lose?

Especially when he stood to gain so much more if he was right and Susie wasn't.

What he wanted to do with this latest return trip to the Lucky C was find something that would negate what Susie was claiming: that that was Greta's blood at the crime scene. That it was Greta's blood that was all over the jagged edges of the broken window.

What possible reason could Greta have for vandalizing the family ranch?

If his sister had a grievance—which would have been news to him—she would have gone to talk to whomever she had the issue with.

Talk to them, not deface their property. For heaven sakes, if anything, Greta had become even closer to the family—certainly closer to their mother—ever since she'd gotten engaged. Greta and their mother were busy planning Greta's *wedding*. She wouldn't just suddenly turn on her mother like that, despite any bizarre tales of hormonal bridezillas to the contrary.

Still, he knew how conscientious Susie was. She wouldn't have just haphazardly conducted that DNA test, or allowed it to become contaminated.

Yet how could her findings be right?

Ryan felt a surge of anger flare up within his chest, anger where his heart was supposed to be.

Try as he might, he couldn't come up with a way that both he and Susie could be right. One of them had to be wrong and he found the idea that it was him really upsetting. *Not* because he had any kind of a problem with his ego—he'd been wrong before, most notably when he'd deployed back overseas and cut Susie loose like that, as if she was some inconvenience instead of someone he had found himself caring for deeply—but because that would mean that there was something seriously bad going on with Greta.

He *knew* Greta. His sister wasn't a criminal. And she didn't harbor some dark side that none of them were aware of. That was just plain ridiculous.

Leaning over, Ryan switched on the radio. The car was instantly filled with the strains of music, instrumental music meant to promote and instill a sense of peace into what was usually a hectic day. He'd never needed it more than he did now.

If he couldn't find evidence at the crime scene that could point him in another direction—the *right* direction—he was going to have to call his sister and question her about the events that had been transpiring here at the ranch. He wasn't looking forward to that because, despite his attempts to keep to himself, he found that he was rather transparent when he was dealing with his family. And once he started questioning Greta about the strange events at the ranch and she realized what he was getting at, there would be a breach between them.

And most likely, between him and the rest of the family, as well. Greta was, after all, the baby of the family, as well as the only girl. Brothers tended to be protective of their little sisters.

Hell, he felt that way, too. But he was also a homicide detective and he had a job to do, a sworn duty to get to the bottom of things and to bring the guilty parties in as well as to protect the innocent ones.

"Damn it, Greta, I sure hope that you're innocent—for both our sakes," he murmured.

And then, because it wasn't affecting him, he turned the music up louder, hoping to be in a better, calmer frame of mind by the time he got back to the Lucky C.

Hoping, but being realistic enough to know that hope alone didn't change a damn thing no matter how much someone might want it to.

Chapter 2

Ryan isn't going to like this.

The thought echoed over and over again in Susie's head as she looked down at the results from the latest DNA test. It was the third such test she'd authorized and this one she'd again done herself. She knew she was wasting her own time, not to mention the lab's precious resources, just to make doubly sure—or triply sure as the case was—that the final results were the same as what had already been concluded the first and second times the test had been run.

There was no mistaking the findings. It was Greta Colton's blood that had been found along the edges of the broken glass from the vandalized stable. It wasn't just a vague familial match, which would have meant that the blood might have belonged to a family member, like Big J or one of Greta's brothers. The match she was looking at was dead-on.

The blood belonged to Greta.

There wasn't a single trace of anyone else's blood on the jagged broken glass. No accomplice, no one else's blood on the scene.

Only Greta's.

Greta had been the one, for whatever reason, who had broken into the stables via the window instead of going in through the door, which as far as she knew, had been Greta's normal custom.

What the hell was going on here?

Why would Greta be breaking into the stables through the window? It just didn't make any sense.

Far from happy, Susie blew out a breath. Much as she really would have preferred coming up with a different conclusion, she had definitely nailed down the who. Now it was up to Ryan to find out the why.

Ryan definitely wasn't going to be happy.

"That did *not* sound like a good sigh."

Perched on a stool against the equipment-laden counter, Susie managed to swivel her stool around to face the doorway. She knew who she would be looking at before she was actually turned around. Nobody else's voice undulated under her skin the way his had.

The way it still did.

Water under the bridge, remember? Water under the bridge. You've moved on. So keep moving, Susie told herself fiercely, albeit silently. Ryan no longer figured into her life, except professionally.

Doing her best to collect herself and look every inch the forensic expert that she was, Susie replied, "It wasn't. And it definitely won't be from your point of view."

Ryan's gut tightened. He knew what was coming and he braced himself—or tried to. "The DNA—"

Susie had never been one to prolong a verdict for the sake of dramatic effect. With distasteful news, it was best to get it out as quickly as possible and move on.

"—is still Greta's," she said, completing his sentence. "I'm sorry, Ryan. I had the test run a total of three times using three different samples from three different areas on the broken glass. I ran two of the tests and had someone else run another one." To back herself up, Susie held up the three separate printouts that had resulted. "It came out the same each and every time. It's Greta's DNA. The blood found at the scene belongs to your sister."

Ryan took the printouts from her and stared at the results on the top sheet. The findings on the two sheets beneath it were identical.

He felt as if someone had driven a knife into his stomach—and was still twisting it.

"There has to be an explanation," he insisted, talking more to himself than to the woman perched on the stool.

"Ask her," Susie suggested matter-of-factly. When Ryan looked down at her with confusion in his eyes, as if he had suddenly realized that he wasn't alone in the room, she said, "If you really think that this doesn't make sense, then ask her why she broke the stable window. Maybe she didn't do it to get into the stables. Maybe there's another plausible reason why the window was broken." And why the stables were vandalized, she added silently.

"You don't believe that," he said, going by the expression on her face.

Susie shrugged away his observation. "What I believe—or don't believe—isn't the point here. I'm the forensic expert, you're the detective. It's up to you to take what I give you and arrange it into some sort of a complete picture that gives you the plausible answers you're looking for."

It almost sounded cut-and-dried—but he knew from experience nothing ever was.

He frowned, looking down at the printout Susie had given him. "This doesn't give me any answers, just more questions."

"It's a start," she told him crisply. "Use it to help you get those answers."

"So now you're telling me my job?" he asked, recalling that she had accused him of doing the same yesterday. He wasn't being defensive, he told himself, just curious to see what the woman would say if he asked. "What is this, a demonstration of 'turnabout is fair play'?"

Maybe she shouldn't have said anything to him, Susie thought. She'd run the tests, done her job and given him the results. It was now up to him to work with what he had. Her part in this was over. She had to keep telling herself that, keep reminding herself to keep her distance, even though something inside her still insisted on holding out the hope that…

That nothing, Susie upbraided herself. There was nothing between them anymore except for business. He'd seen to that.

"Just trying to make the results more palatable for you, Detective Colton," she told him.

Ryan winced. He could almost feel the frost encrusted around her words. "Ouch. That's pretty formal. But I guess I deserve that."

Yes, you do. That and a hell of a lot more, she added silently. "See, you're detecting already," she told him, doing her best to keep distancing herself from Ryan. She knew if she didn't, if she allowed just a crack to open up, no matter how small, he'd somehow seep into her system, and just like that she'd be vulnerable all over again. In danger of having her heart ripped out again. She'd been down that route once and had no desire to revisit it. "Now, if you don't mind, I've got cases other than yours all clamoring for my time…" She allowed her voice to drift off as she deliberately made a show of getting back to work.

"No. Sure. Thanks." The single-word sentences came out of his mouth in staccato fashion, as if he was firing each word one by one, pausing in between each.

She heard Ryan begin to walk toward the exit. This was where she was supposed to continue looking down at the work on her desk, the work she was already supposed to have finished but had moved aside so that she could run those additional DNA tests in hopes of finding another suspect, one that wasn't Ryan's sister.

All she had to do was hold out a total of thirty seconds. Fifty, tops, and he would be gone, Susie told herself.

There was really no need for her to say anything more to the man than she'd already said.

No need at all—except, perhaps, to satisfy her own curiosity about a man she had once believed herself to be madly in love with.

Once?

Hell, you're still in love with him, you big idiot. You think you would've learned by now, Susie upbraided herself, annoyed at her own lack of discipline, not to mention a certain dearth of self-respect.

But for her internal lectures never took, no matter how driven they were by common sense, and she found herself turning all the way around on her stool.

She was just in time to see Ryan about to step over the threshold, out into the hall.

Two more seconds and she'd be home free.

One—

"So what are you going to do?" she heard herself asking Ryan.

Apparently already lost in thought, Ryan jerked his head up. He'd heard her voice, but not the words that she'd said. "What?"

"So what are you going to do?" Susie repeated, enunciating each word.

Ryan crossed back over the threshold, but only took a couple of steps toward her before he stopped. He had to admit he was surprised that she was interested enough to ask him that. "I'm going to call Greta and do just what you suggested. I'm going to ask her what she was doing in the stable and why she had to break the window in order to get in."

Susie thought for a moment. "Your sister's a horse trainer, isn't she?"

He was surprised that Susie had taken the time to find that out. It wasn't as if they ran in the same circles these days. And back when they were together, their worlds had contained only each other, to the exclusion of everyone else. That meant family members, as well.

"Best in the business," Ryan confirmed.

"Maybe she was passing by the stable at that hour for some reason, looked in and thought she saw smoke coming from the stable. Or maybe she thought she saw a horse in distress. The fastest way from point A to point B is still a straight line." She shrugged carelessly, unable to come up with any better explanations at the moment. "Maybe that was why she broke the window."

Although he appreciated her effort, he thought that Susie was definitely reaching. "And she didn't stick around to tell anyone what she did?" Ryan asked skeptically.

Susie took her theory to the next step. "She was probably too embarrassed about breaking the window for no reason so she didn't hang around, waiting for someone from the family to hear her out. Most likely, she's just working up the nerve to answer for what she did. Nobody likes to admit that they made a mistake or acted rashly," she pointed out.

They were talking about his sister, and Susie was giving him ammunition to defend Greta's actions, but he really wasn't convinced.

"I suppose that sounds plausible enough," he allowed. "But I'll believe it when I hear it from Greta's own lips. Last I heard, she's not even supposed to be in Tulsa right now."

"Well, *she* might not be, but her blood certainly is," Susie said, indicating the printouts he was holding. "I don't have to point out that you can't have one without the other."

"Unless someone's trying to frame you," Ryan

said as the idea suddenly occurred to him. The only thing that wasn't occurring to him was why someone would go to the sort of trouble that actually framing his sister would require.

But even as he began to vaguely entertain the idea, he saw Susie shaking her head.

Exasperation seeped into his tone. "What?" he asked.

She had to stop him before he got carried away with the idea he seemed to be embracing. "If someone for some obscure reason actually *did* manage to have a sample of your sister's blood—and I'm talking about enough to smear on the jagged edges of the window—it would have started to coagulate in a vial. There are certain characteristics of stored blood that would have shown up in the blood workup that was done. They didn't," she informed him flatly. "This blood was fresh when it came in contact with the broken glass."

"I was afraid of that," he murmured, again more to himself than to her.

Susie's slender shoulders rose and fell, not in a show of indifference, but to signify that some things just couldn't be changed no matter how much one might want them to be different.

"So, go back to your initial plan," she told him.

"Which was?" he asked, wanting to see what Susie thought his plan had been.

"You said you were going to go question your sister and ask Greta what she was doing there at that time of night. Ask her why she thought it was necessary to break into stables that she could have just as easily accessed the proper way—through the door."

Susie was right of course. But the more he thought about it, the more this proposed conversation with Greta was *not* going to be a conversation that he was looking forward to. Added to that was the fact that Greta had been a little jumpy since their mother had been found battered and beaten.

In the past couple of months his normally cheerful little sister had become increasingly uneasy, at times acting almost paranoid, and questioning her about the acts of vandalism and the break-in at the Lucky C was definitely *not* going to help the situation *or* Greta's frame of mind, he thought.

He could feel Susie's eyes on him, as if scrutinizing his very thought process. What she said next all but confirmed his suspicions.

"Maybe you should take another family member with you when you go to question her," Susie suggested.

Susie pressed her lips together. She knew she should just keep out of this. After all, the man had all but callously torn her heart right out of her chest without so much as a warning shot. She owed him nothing.

But even so, the look on his face had her feeling for him. She knew that if she were in his place, confronting this sort of situation, she would feel awful.

Memories from the past tried to break through, memories of a time when they were each other's entire world.

But that was then, this was now, she reminded herself. She had to get a grip on her emotions. They had absolutely no place here.

"Thanks," he said, surprised that Susie would even bother to attempt to give him helpful suggestions, given their past. "But that's not a good idea. If I take one of my brothers with me, Greta will think we're ganging up on her. She's been on edge ever since our mother was attacked." He remembered being called to the scene by his frantic father and racing to his mother's side. The whole episode was vividly imprinted on his mind.

"Just before she slipped into an unconscious state, when I asked my mother who did this to her, she just stared at me and then started to cry. I couldn't get her to say anything or even indicate whether or not she had seen the attacker's face. She slipped into a coma right after that.

"When she finally came out of her coma, every time Greta was anywhere near her, my mother looked, I don't know, *spooked* I guess is the best word for it. As for Greta, she just looked uncomfortable—and hurt." He shrugged helplessly. "I don't know what to make of any of it."

For a moment Susie forgot that she wasn't supposed to be talking to Ryan beyond uttering a few monosyllabic responses. All she saw was an all-too-human homicide detective, torn between job responsibilities and familial loyalties—a fellow human being in need of some kind of support.

That was the Ryan she was talking to.

"If not another family member, maybe you could take another female with you to be supportive of Greta as well as you," she proposed.

"You?" Ryan asked in surprise. Was she actually offering to come with him to question Greta?

Susie shrugged. She had painted herself into a corner with that one, she thought. The focus wasn't supposed to be on her but on the situation—and the crime. She'd meant the suggestion in a general way, but there was no denying that she *was* a female.

"I do qualify for the category," she was forced to admit, almost against her will.

Ryan smiled then, remembering a time prior to the breakup he had engineered. A time when everything had seemed perfect despite the claim the service had on him. Remembering a very small island of time when he had been in love, and had just allowed things to "be" without any in-depth analysis.

"If memory serves me, you more than qualify—and thanks for offering—but this is something I have to do on my own," he told her. "I think that the less people Greta sees when I arrive, the better this whole situation might work out."

Or at least that was what he hoped.

Susie didn't know if he was just being protective of his sister, or if Ryan was once again dismissing her wholesale out of his life.

In either case, she told herself, her conscience was clear. Despite the extenuating circumstances, she'd offered to do the right thing. That she had done so was not negated by his refusal of her offer. It just made her square with him.

"Suit yourself," she responded, doing what she could to sound indifferent. "You always know best."

The last part had sounded incredibly cold as well as formal and withdrawn to his ear. Whatever bridge they had crossed a moment ago was now officially uncrossed again and they were back to their initial corners. They were once again on the opposite sides of the fence, the words *opposite sides* all but ten feet tall with neon lights dancing around them.

He didn't have time for this, didn't have time to deal with any regrets, small or, in this case, large. What was done was done and he had to focus on the present. Just possibly, he had a sister to bring back to the fold. A sister that he had to take care not to alienate as he tried to subtly question her about her part—if she *had* played a part—in these bizarre, random attacks of vandalism and destruction that were occurring on the ranch.

A sister who just might never forgive him if she proved to be innocent of any wrongdoing and thought that he was accusing her of the exact opposite.

There were times when he scolded himself for not having chosen a simpler, easier path in life. But everyone had to follow their strengths, he reasoned, and his involved ferreting out the truth and taking down the bad guys.

"Thanks for all your help," he said to Susie as he started to leave again.

She looked up at him. "I'm sure you don't mean that, but you're welcome."

He was about to take exception with the way she had phrased that—it sounded as if she had stopped just short of calling him a liar—but he caught himself just in time. There was no point in attempting to contradict her point of view about the immediate matter at hand. She had a right to her opinion, even if she was dead wrong. Because he *had* meant what he'd just said.

He was deliberately wasting time. Every minute he stood here was another minute that he was delaying the inevitable because it was going to be, at best, awkward and uncomfortable. He didn't want to think about what it would be like at its worst.

Squaring his shoulders, he left the lab. He needed to get this over with. Now.

And then, he thought as he went down the corridor, he could move on to something else.

Hopefully more successfully than the last time he'd told himself he was moving on.

He sincerely doubted that he could do any worse.

Chapter 3

Ryan knew that as an investigating detective with the Tulsa PD, even if he was questioning his own sister, because he was doing it in reference to a current active case he was working on, it was in everyone's best interest to keep things businesslike and official. Among other things, that meant that he should be making this call from the phone on his desk at the precinct, not from his personal cell phone while he was sitting in his car.

He supposed that he could argue that he was doing it for the quiet, because the precinct was usually almost too noisy to allow anyone to hear themselves think. But the truth of the matter was that his real reason for making the call from inside his vehicle was that he didn't want to be overheard.

It was bad enough that he had to ask his sister painful, probing questions like this without having everyone within a ten-foot radius *hearing* him asking. He was a Colton. One of *the* Coltons. The family that had, through absolutely no fault of their own, their very own serial killer in their family tree, thanks to his father's brother, Matthew.

Granted, it all had happened a long time ago and his uncle had been locked away in prison for a while now, but he was well aware of the fact that people loved to point an accusing finger and watch people of prominence come tumbling down. They loved watching their fallen-from-grace sinners every bit as much as they loved cheering on their saints and heroes.

Sometimes even more so.

He wanted no part in supplying those people with any sort of ammunition, especially if there did actually turn out to be a reasonable excuse for all this.

He supposed a tiny part of him hadn't turned cynical yet and still believed in miracles.

So he sat in his vehicle, trying not to notice how stuffy it seemed with the windows rolled up and his doors locked, and he called his sister's number.

After a short delay, he heard the cell phone start to ring. Waiting for Greta to answer her phone, Ryan counted off the number of times her cell rang. After four, her voice mail kicked in. Impatient, he was about to terminate the call and try again in a couple of minutes when he heard Greta's breathless voice as she came on the line.

"Hello?"

Rather than relax, he felt his shoulders stiffen. "Greta? It's me. Ryan."

"Hi." And then he heard her ask guardedly, "What's up?"

Was that just his imagination—or her guilty conscience stepping up? "I'm coming up to the ranch to see you."

He heard her laugh softly. "Well, you can come up to the ranch, but you won't see me."

Was he tipping her off with this call? Was she planning on taking off? He needed more to work with. "Why?" he asked.

"Why do you think?" Not waiting for him to respond, she gave him the answer to her own question. "Because I'm not at the ranch. I'm not in Tulsa at all. I'm back in Oklahoma City."

Ryan frowned to himself. Ever since Greta had gotten engaged, she'd spent more and more of her time in Oklahoma City, where her fiancé lived. She'd even taken on horse training jobs there.

"I thought you'd stick around the ranch for a while, you know, because of Mother."

There was silence on the other end of the line and for a moment, he thought that the call had been dropped. But then Greta said, "Yes, well, I wasn't really doing her any good just hanging around the house. Especially since she kept looking at me as if she was afraid of me. As if she thought I was going to do something to her. I don't know what's with that," Greta complained, sounding as if she was at a complete loss.

"Did you ask her about it?" Ryan asked.

"Yes. But when I asked her why she was looking at me like that," Greta went on, obviously upset about the matter, "she denied it."

"So what's the problem?"

He heard Greta sigh. "I got the feeling she denied it because she was afraid if she didn't, I'd do something to her."

He couldn't believe that things between his mother and sister had actually degenerated down to this, but then Abra was prone to mood swings. "You're imagining things, Greta."

He heard Greta sigh. "I suppose that maybe I am, but just the other day she asked me if I was doing any recreational drugs. Me, who's never taken anything stronger than an aspirin. I think that beating Mother took might have been even more serious than any of us suspected."

It was Ryan's turn to sigh. No one was more frustrated about not being able to find whoever had hurt his mother than he was. But right now, he had the break-in to deal with.

The break-in with the evidence mounting against Greta. There *had* to be an explanation for all this, he thought, but he needed to talk to her in person to get at the truth.

Growing up, Greta had been a tomboy almost in self-defense. She'd been outnumbered by her brothers five to one and had learned to hold her own at a very early age. At five-nine she was tall and willowy, and at first glance, very feminine.

But she was also tough to the point that he was certain no one could easily push her around. As far as he knew, his sister didn't really have much of a temper, but then he supposed everyone could be pushed to their limit. What was Greta's limit? he couldn't help wondering.

Was there something that could push Greta over the edge?

His thought process suddenly took him in a very new direction, almost against his will. What if, for some reason, their mother had suddenly taken exception to Greta's pending marriage to Mark Stanton? Handsome and glibly charming, it was no secret that the younger brother of the president of Stanton Oil got by on his looks, not his work ethic. Maybe, despite the fact that she had been instrumental in throwing Greta and Mark an engagement party— their father always left such things to his wife— Abra had told Greta to slow down and think things through and Greta had balked. One thing could have had led to another and—

And what? Ryan silently demanded. Greta had had a complete reversal in personality and gone ballistic on their mother? That account just didn't fly for him.

None of this was making any sense to him—and he was getting one hell of a headache just reviewing all the various details over and over again in his head.

"Ryan? Are you still there?" The stress in Greta's voice broke through his thoughts.

"What?" Embarrassed, he flushed. Luckily there was no one to see him. "Yeah, I'm still here, Greta. How long have you been in Oklahoma City?" he asked her abruptly, changing direction.

He heard her hesitate. Was she thinking, or...?

"A couple of weeks or so," Greta finally answered. "Why?"

Ryan suppressed his sigh. "Which is it? A couple of weeks? Or 'so'?"

"Three weeks," she replied more specifically, irritation evident in her voice. "Just what's this all about, Ryan?"

He didn't address her question. Instead, he asked her another one of his own. "So you weren't there—at the ranch—yesterday morning? Or the night before?"

"No, I already told you," she replied, annoyed. "I was here, working. Why are you asking me all these weird questions?" she asked. And then, as if she had a premonition about what was happening, she asked, "Ryan, what's going on?"

He gave her the unvarnished details. "Someone broke into the stables early yesterday morning."

"That's awful," she cried, upset. And then realization entered her voice, as did abject horror. "Wait, why would you think that it was me?"

Maybe he should have refrained from telling her this until later, but Greta *was* his sister and he had to give her every benefit of the doubt. "Because one of the windows had been deliberately broken and there was blood on the jagged edges."

Even as she said the words, she couldn't really get herself to believe it. It was there in her voice as she asked in stunned disbelief, "My blood?"

He had never hated sharing a piece of information more than this. "Yes."

She felt as if she had slipped into some sort of parallel universe, one that was not bound by the laws of reason—or reality for that matter.

Stunned, she protested, "That's not possible," because she couldn't see how it could be. "What reason would I have to break into the stable, going through a window for heaven's sake?" she demanded.

"I don't know, Greta. That's what I'm trying to find out," he told her wearily. "The DNA test that came back from the lab was conclusive."

"Then you need better equipment—or better people doing the test—because the results they came up with are *wrong*. I wasn't there," Greta insisted heatedly one more time. "I was here, in Oklahoma City, working with the horses."

Ryan paused for a moment, hating what he had to ask. But this was protocol, not something personal—even though he knew that Greta would take it that way. And in her place, he would have felt the same way. "Can anyone vouch for you?"

"The horses aren't talking," she snapped at him in exasperation.

"I didn't think so," he replied, hoping to inject a tiny trace of humor into the extremely awkward exchange. "How about the rancher who hired you?"

"Sorry, no help in that quarter," she informed her brother coldly. "He's away on business. Apparently *he* trusts me because I've got free access to his ranch while he's away so I can come and go at will."

Ryan took no offense at the attitude that had slipped into his sister's voice. If someone had been listening to their exchange, it would sound as if he was trying to break Greta down.

"How about Mark?" he asked hopefully. Personally, he didn't care for his sister's intended, but maybe the man could prove good for something. Maybe he could provide the alibi that Greta needed. "Is he—"

Greta cut him off. "Mark's just away. I don't know where he is."

What she didn't say was that her fiancé had been rather flaky of late, not showing up when he said he would, being secretive whenever he did show up. She had a very uneasy feeling that the second she had agreed to marry him, Mark had decided he no longer had to be on his best behavior.

But none of this was something she wanted to share with her family, especially since someone had almost killed her mother, and apparently her police detective brother thought that she might be the one who was responsible for that.

Ryan jumped on the last thing she'd said like a hungry dog on his first bone after suffering a week of deprivation. "What do you mean you don't know where he is?"

Greta's tone became entirely defensive. It was obvious that she was tired of having to defend herself. "Just what I said. He's my fiancé, Ryan, not my pet. I don't keep track of him when he's 'off leash,'" she informed her brother heatedly.

Ryan felt he would have had to have been deaf to have missed her hostility. Not that he could blame her. Again, he supposed he'd feel the same way in her place if she'd all but accused him of hurting their mother and then began questioning him about vandalizing the family ranch.

The Lucky C was their father's pride and joy. Big J treated the ranch as if it was actually an entity unto itself, as human as the rest of them—at times, maybe even more so.

Much as he hated to admit it, he had lost control

of this conversation. All he'd wanted to do was arrange to get together with Greta to have this discussion face-to-face and it had veered completely off track. He had no idea how to smooth things over, only that he had to do it in order to get something to work with.

Pausing, he searched for words. But before they could come to him, his cell buzzed, announcing a second call was attempting to come in.

The phrase "saved by the bell" suddenly occurred to him.

"Hold on a minute, Greta, I've got another call coming in."

He could almost hear her sign of relief. "Take your call, Ryan. I've got to go," she told him a beat before the line went dead.

Frustrated, Ryan blew out a breath. He'd just been about to tell her to remain on the line but she had hung up before he had the chance.

He tried not to read anything incriminating into Greta's quick and abrupt withdrawal. If need be, he'd get Susie's rather annoying intern to pinpoint Greta's exact location to make doubly sure that his sister was actually where she said she was. Armed with that information, he could determine just where she was staying so he could drive to Oklahoma City and bring his sister back if he needed to.

He hated this.

What he hated even more was that he had a very

strong hunch that "needed to" was going to turn out to be a reality, and soon.

Very soon.

"Colton," he announced as he took the incoming call.

"You better get out here, boy," a shaken voice instructed him.

For one isolated moment, Ryan didn't recognize the voice. But he could be forgiven for that since he had never heard his father sounding this way. Stunned. Numb. And battling complete disbelief—as well as sounding just the tiniest bit fearful.

"Dad?" Ryan asked, still only half-certain that he was right.

"Yeah, it's me." His father's voice, usually so bombastic and full of life, sounded incredibly old. "Get out here as quick as you can, Ryan. And come *alone*," his father added, emphasizing the last word.

"More vandalism?" Ryan asked wearily. He'd had just about enough drama to last for a while.

"No," his father snapped, dismissing the question as inconsequential. "It's bad."

Okay, Ryan thought. This sounded serious. And personal. He could only think of one thing that would prompt his father to evaluate the situation this way. "Is it Mother?" he asked, even as he prayed— something he hadn't done in more years than he could remember—that it wasn't.

"No. No, it's not Abra," his father was quick to say. "But you have to get out here."

The urgency in his father's voice was unnerving. There was a time when their father had them all intimidated. John Colton was a big man who cast a large shadow and had a voice like gravel.

"Then what is it?" Ryan asked. Now that he thought about it, his father almost sounded spooked. If this didn't involve his mother, why did his father sound like he was frightened?

"Damn it, Ryan, I can't talk about this over the phone. What good is it having a police detective in the family if I have to argue with you every time I need you to handle something for me? Just get out here, Ryan," his father ordered. *"Now."*

He knew better than to think that his father was playing games. Something else had happened on the ranch and rather than wasting time trying to get his father to tell him what was going on, he needed to see this for himself.

"Where's 'here,' Dad?" he asked.

"The ranch, of course," Big J retorted. "You suddenly gone dumb on me?"

Ryan didn't bother answering that. "It's big ranch, Dad. *Where* on the ranch? The main house, the Cabin, what?"

The main house was where his parents lived, along with Brett, his wife and Greta when she was in Tulsa. Jack, his wife and his son lived in what had once been the main house until the new one had been built, while Daniel and Megan lived in what everyone just referred to as "the Cabin." That, too, was located on the ranch.

"Come to the bunkhouse," his father instructed in a voice that was almost eerily still.

After terminating the call, Ryan tossed his cell phone onto the passenger seat and started up his vehicle.

Given the situation, the logical thing would have been to bring backup with him, especially since his father had sounded so shaken up, an unusual state of affairs when it came to Big J.

But since his father had also been adamant no one else come to the ranch to see this—whatever "this" was—except for him, Ryan felt as if he had to go with his father's instincts.

Besides, *his* instincts told him to play this very close to his vest—at least until he knew what the hell was going on.

Ryan paused only long enough to reach into his glove compartment to take out his vehicle's emergency-light attachment. Switching it on, he placed the whirling red and yellow lights onto his roof, securing it. Once he had, he hit the gas and took off.

Ryan did between eighty and ninety all the way to the ranch, something he would have loved to have done as a teenager. He would have enjoyed it a lot more then than now.

Once he reached the ranch, he took the long way around to the bunkhouse, passing all the other buildings just in case his father had been addled when he'd told him where to go. Ryan assumed that if that was the case, he would see his father standing in front of whatever structure he'd actually meant to direct him toward.

But Big J was not out in front of the main house.

Or the old main house.

Or the Cabin.

The process of elimination told him that his father had really meant to direct him to the bunkhouse.

Why was his father being so melodramatic? Was this actually just another break-in, complete with its own acts of vandalism?

This was definitely getting old, Ryan thought as he headed toward the bunkhouse.

His father was waiting for him out front.

Ryan could make out the lines etched in his father's face. They were evident even at this distance.

After pulling up in front of the bunkhouse, Ryan got out of his vehicle. Maybe this wouldn't be as bad as his father was making it sound.

"Okay, what's the big emergency?" Ryan asked his father as he approached.

"This way," was all his father said as he gestured for Ryan to follow him into the bunkhouse.

"What the hell is all this mystery about?" Ryan asked impatiently.

"You'll see," Big J told him grimly.

Walking behind his father as they entered the building, Ryan thought that he was pretty much prepared for anything.

But he was wrong.

Chapter 4

There was a dead man lying on his back in the center of the bunkhouse floor, a drying pool of blood beneath him, a surprised look frozen on his young face.

Whatever he had expected to find when his father had summoned him, deliberately refraining from giving him any details, it definitely hadn't been this.

Ryan felt as if he was moving in slow motion as he circled the prone body of the young cowboy with the conspicuous hole in his chest. He was careful not to step into or otherwise disturb the wide pool of blood that had had at least several hours to seep out of the man's body.

Only after he had completely circumvented the

ranch hand's—Kurt Rodgers's—earthly remains did Ryan squat down beside him.

Rodgers's complexion was already beginning to take on a grayish pallor. That, and the condition of the blood on the floor, indicated that the cowboy had been dead for a while.

Even so, Ryan pulled out the handkerchief he had tucked into the back pocket of his jeans and gingerly felt along the cowboy's throat and neck for any sign of a pulse.

There was none.

He hadn't really expected one, but there was always that wild, outside chance that the man might have somehow still been clinging to life. Ryan felt he couldn't rule that possibility out until he'd made absolutely sure.

Ryan caught himself thinking that the victim— a fairly recent hire who had an affinity for horses and had helped Greta and Daniel train the ranch's horses—looked awfully young.

Just yesterday, Kurt's whole life had been ahead of him. And now, it wasn't.

Ryan was aware that his father had crept closer during the cursory exam and now hovered around him, peering over his shoulder. "That's Kurt Rodgers," Big J said.

Ryan didn't bother looking his way. "I know who it is, Dad."

Big J shrugged in response. "It's just that lately,

unless you're investigating something going on at the Lucky C, you're never here."

Rising, Ryan pocketed his handkerchief. Irritation filled his voice. "I said I know who it is. Sorry," he apologized the next moment.

He wasn't annoyed with his father but with this latest, far more serious turn of events. Was this just a random murder or one that involved his family?

"It's just that checking out a dead body in my family's bunkhouse isn't exactly something I ever expected to be doing." Taking a breath, he looked around the otherwise empty bunkhouse. "Who found him?"

"Brett," his father answered. At twenty-eight, Brett was the youngest of the Colton brothers. "Near as I can figure, he was coming in from one of his late-night work sessions," Big J explained. "Boy was all white when he came and got me—I couldn't sleep and was in the study," his father added as an afterthought. "Brett looked like he'd seen a ghost or something."

"Or something," Ryan repeated, stifling a frustrated sigh. "Was anyone else with him at the time?" Ryan asked.

Big J guessed at what his son was really asking him. "You mean was Hannah with him? If she was, she took off before anyone else saw her. As far as I know, he was alone when he saw Rodgers lying there like that." He shook his head sadly as he looked down at his murdered employee.

Ryan absently nodded, jotting down key points from his father's statement. "Where's Brett now?"

"At the house, most likely trying to steady his nerves." A vague shrug accompanied his father's words, as if he wasn't a hundred percent certain that his youngest son was still where he just said he was. "I gave him my best Kentucky bourbon."

Ryan rolled his eyes. "Great, just what I need. An intoxicated witness to question."

"He's not a witness," Big J countered defensively, as if the term was somehow tainted, or would taint anyone it came in contact with. "He's your brother."

Ryan didn't see why that fact should create a discrepancy in the description. "Who was also the first one who found the body, that makes him a witness—of the scene, since he wasn't here for the commission of the crime." Ryan assumed that his father would have said as much if Brett had seen who had killed the ranch hand. "Was there anyone else here at the time?" he asked, rephrasing his previous question.

"Like I said, not that I saw," Big J answered. "I called you the minute I saw Rodgers lying there like that."

Ryan pressed his lips together, far from happy about this turn of events—or the predicament it would most likely put him in. What if, for some reason, another one of his siblings was behind this, or at least somehow connected to this?

It hadn't been a great week for family relations, he couldn't help thinking.

Reaching into his other back pocket, Ryan pulled out his cell phone. As he did so, he waved his father back. "You can't be here right now."

Full, bushy eyebrows drew together over Big J's patrician nose. "Why not?" the big man demanded, for the moment sounding every bit like his former, larger-than-life self. "This is my bunkhouse, boy."

"Nobody's disputing that, Dad," Ryan replied. "But right now it's my crime scene, and until it's processed, that tops your claim to it."

"Possession's nine-tenths of the law and I've got the deed, boy." Although he was proud of his sons, Big J was not about to be easily usurped. He was the head of the family. "Okay, okay," Big J said, raising his hands defensively when Ryan looked at him darkly, giving no sign of backing down. "I'll get on out."

John Colton began to do just that when he stopped suddenly to take a closer look at his son's face, as if he was trying to gauge the gravity of what was transpiring on his property.

"Should I be calling Preston?" he asked, referring to David Preston, the fifty-year-old lawyer who he kept on retainer to handle any legal matters involving either him or his family.

"Not yet, Dad. But it wouldn't hurt to let him know what's going on," Ryan told him.

His father began to say something in response to that, but Ryan raised his hand, stopping him. The phone on the other end of the call he was making had stopped ringing and had been picked up.

A melodic, albeit preoccupied female voice announced, "Crime lab."

Susie.

Because his father was standing not that far off, despite his instructions to the contrary, Ryan addressed the woman he had called—the woman he had once made love to with abandon—formally.

"This is Detective Ryan Colton. I need the CSI unit to come out to the Lucky C."

The impatient exhale echoed in his ear as he heard Susie say, "Look, I understand how you feel, Colton, but we just don't have time to run a fourth DNA test on that broken window," she told him in a voice that declared that there would be no further discussions on the matter.

"This isn't about the broken window," Ryan said sharply, cutting in before she had the opportunity to continue.

There was a long pause on the other end, as if the forensic expert was debating whether or not she believed him. "Then what?" she finally asked.

"We've got a body at the bunkhouse," he answered grimly.

"Do you know who it is?" she asked him.

Ryan thought he heard rustling on the other end

of the line, like she was getting her evidence case together to bring to the crime scene. "Yeah, it's one of the ranch hands, a relatively new hire named Kurt Rodgers."

"Are there signs of a struggle?" Susie asked.

Ryan turned around to look at the area around the cowboy's body. The only thing that appeared out of place was Rodgers's body itself—and the pool of blood beneath it, that went without saying. Nothing else seemed to be disturbed.

"From all indications, he didn't see whatever it was coming," Ryan answered. "Send your people out here."

"Right away," she promised, snapping the locks on her case.

Ryan thought that was the end of their conversation and was about to terminate the call when he heard Susie's voice.

"Ryan?"

He put the phone back up to his ear. "Yeah?" He saw his father looking at him, as if Big J was trying to ascertain what was going on.

Her voice softened just a touch as she told him, "I'm sorry."

Ryan didn't have to ask about what. He knew. Susie was telling him that she was sorry he was going through this. It was hard enough investigating a murder, but when the murder took place on his own family's ranch, that added an extra dimension to the case. A dimension that made it almost too delicate to work on, at least for him.

"Thanks," he told her, adding, "Me, too."

With that, Ryan ended the call and tucked his cell phone back into his pocket. He knew he was going to have to call his boss, Boyd Benson, who was the Tulsa chief of police, and tell him what was going on. The man wouldn't be happy about this. But then, in all fairness, he had no idea what *did* make the police chief happy. Benson's regular expression was a dour one. Ryan couldn't recall ever seeing the man smile, not even at one of the Christmas parties.

Now that he thought about it, he'd never seen the man actually attend a Christmas party. The chief was fair and honest, but not exactly a pleasure to get along with.

Ryan put off calling Benson for a few minutes, giving himself time to nail down exactly what he would tell his boss when he called him. Benson preferred having the maximum amount of information delivered to him using the minimum number of words.

"'You, too' what?" Big J asked the moment he saw his son putting his phone away.

Caught off guard, Ryan could only eye his father quizzically. "What?"

"That person you called, the one you told to send that crime scene unit of yours out here, you said 'me, too' when he or she said something to you," Big J said. "I'm just asking what you were talking about."

He supposed it would do no harm to fill his father in on something that was innocuous. "The forensic expert said she was sorry you were going through this." Okay, so he had reworded it, but he thought it might make the situation a bit more palatable for his father if Big J thought the head of the crime lab sympathized. "And just so you understand, it isn't *my* crime scene unit. It's the police department's crime scene unit."

"But you're part of the police department, aren't you?" his father pressed doggedly.

Ryan could see where this was going. Nonetheless, he played along. "You know I am."

"Then it's *your* crime scene unit," Big J concluded triumphantly.

Ryan paused. It wasn't very hard to read between the lines. "Dad, this isn't a matter of you and I being on opposite sides of this investigation."

Big J became defensive. "Yeah, I know. I was the one who called you and told you to come here in the first place, remember?"

"Yes, Dad," Ryan replied, doing his best to remain patient, or at least to sound as if he was being patient. "I remember." There were times when he wished he'd never left the Marines. He had a feeling that this would soon be one of those times. "I'm going to tape off the crime scene and then talk to Brett," he told his father, knowing that the man wanted to be kept abreast of everything that was going on.

Though it was far from standard procedure, he was trying his best to keep Big J informed, hoping that would be enough to keep his father in the background rather than hovering front and center.

"But this is the bunkhouse," Big J protested. "You can't go 'taping' it off. I've got people sleeping here at night."

He really felt as if they were butting heads at every turn. And the man wasn't dumb. He knew better, yet he kept challenging him.

"You're going to have to make other arrangements for them for the time being, Dad. I'll try to get this processed as soon as possible, but until that happens, your ranch hands are going to have to sleep somewhere else."

He saw that the information left his father slightly confused for a moment. He hated seeing that because that was a sign of the creeping dementia that was slowly laying siege to and overtaking his father's mind.

It was hard for either one of them to become reconciled to that hard fact. Big J had always been a vital presence and the thought of his father being any less vital, of being diminished in any way, was difficult for Ryan to accept.

It had to be twice as hard for his father.

Nonetheless, Ryan had become aware that sometimes the most logical of thought processes could escape his father for a moment, if not longer.

Life was nothing if not cruel, he couldn't help thinking.

"How about having them stay at the old house?" Ryan suggested patiently.

If his father noticed the shift in tone, he wasn't letting on. Instead, Big J commented on his suggestion. "Jack's not going to like that."

The old main house, as Ryan thought of it, was where his oldest brother, John Jr.; Tracy, his wife; and Ryan's nephew, five-year-old Seth, currently called home. The boy was the proverbial apple of everyone's eye and the one continuing bright spot as all these mishaps kept on occurring.

"Maybe," Ryan agreed. "But Seth's going to be thrilled. He'll get all these new 'playmates,'" he pointed out to his father.

It was no secret that the ranch hands all doted on the boy. They took turns teaching him various things that would come in handy for him as he grew older and took a bigger part in working on the ranch alongside his father, uncles and aunt.

Right now, the boy was half kid, half mascot, Ryan mused.

And all energy, he silently added, wishing, not for the first time, that he could find a way to tap into that energy, at least for a little while.

Going to his car, Ryan took out the yellow crime

scene tape. So armed, he wrapped the tape around the entire exterior of the bunkhouse, making sure that the front door would be accessible to Susie and her team when they arrived.

He was beginning to really hate the color yellow, he thought, putting what was left of the roll back into his vehicle.

"Okay, take me to Brett," he told his father. "I need to question him.

For a moment, his father remained exactly where he was. "You sure about this, son?" he questioned. "Brett's been through a lot already. It's his first dead body," Big J reminded him.

Ryan gently but firmly herded his father toward his car. "Yeah, I'm sure. I need to find out if he saw something and just what the crime scene was like when he got there. Nothing looks like it was moved, but…" His voice trailed off.

"You want to be sure," Big J guessed.

"I want to be sure," Ryan reiterated. "And as for Brett, with any luck at all, he'll never see another dead body again."

"Amen to that, boy," his father said as he got into the passenger seat of the sedan.

Ryan wished he could say the same thing for himself, but the job he had signed on for didn't just require him to handle the pristine cases. He dealt with them all. The only thing that gave him a measure of comfort was the fact that if he were the law in some tiny town where the biggest excitement involved getting a treed cat back down on solid ground, he'd most likely go insane from the acute boredom within a month.

However, that didn't negate the fact that every once in a while he would really like things to go smoothly and peacefully for more than a couple of days at a time.

Reaching the main house, Ryan left his vehicle parked out front. Even though he was as familiar with the layout of the house as his father was, he allowed Big J to lead the way.

"There he is," Big J announced, standing just short of the threshold leading into the formal dining room.

Brett was sitting at the table, one hand still firmly wrapped around the bourbon bottle his father had given him. His face was flat against the tabletop and he looked, for all intents and purposes, to be dead to the world. With work, a wife and a new baby on the way, he had to be down for the count.

At least temporarily.

Ryan walked up to his younger brother and gave waking him up one try. He shook Brett's shoulder.

Brett made no response, other than to snore loudly for a total of thirty seconds. After that, as Ryan backed away, his brother's breathing returned to a steadier, softer cadence.

"I'm not getting anything out of him for at least a few hours," Ryan concluded.

If then, he added silently. With that, he left the main house and went back to the bunkhouse to wait for the crime scene unit.

Chapter 5

Susie felt torn.

Torn between hiding behind the safety of her position at the crime lab—thus allowing her to keep as much distance between herself and the man who had skewered her heart ten years ago—and going out to the crime scene with her team and personally working it. If she did the latter, she would most likely all but trip over Ryan Colton.

There had been a time, ten years ago, when she would have eagerly welcomed the second scenario. But ten years ago, she had been starry-eyed and incredibly naive. She had been desperately, *desperately* in love with the six-foot-two, muscular, green-eyed, dark-haired Marine from the very first moment she had laid eyes on him. And, from the way he had acted, she had been certain that the feeling was mutual. Certain that they would love one another forever—or for as long as their forever lasted. At the time, she'd thought that would be the next fifty, sixty years, which just showed how very naive she'd been back then because in their case, "forever" had an incredibly short life span.

When Ryan had told her the news that he was being deployed overseas again, she'd been upset— who wouldn't be?—but she promised that she would wait for him no matter how long it took. Love to her meant taking the bad times with the good. It meant staying home and praying for his safe return while her Marine went off to fight. It meant patience and waiting.

However, it apparently meant none of those things to Ryan. For him, the key phrase was "out of sight, out of mind" and it was applicable to love, because she had obviously faded from his mind the very moment he had left American soil.

His letter to her had said as much, if not in so many words. By any standards, what he'd written had been an exceedingly harsh breakup letter without an iota of tenderness to it.

She kept the letter, not for any sentimental reason but to remind her, should she ever be tempted to give away her heart again, *not to*. Not unless she wanted to be the less-than-proud owner of a trampled heart for a second time.

Once was more than enough for her, and although the incident had happened ten years ago it still felt like only yesterday—but never so vividly as four years ago when she saw Ryan walking down the PD hallway, headed in her direction.

Only later, after they had both recovered the use of their tongues—he, of course, faster than she—did it come to light that they were both working for the Tulsa police department, he as a homicide detective and she in the forensic lab, something that had always interested her.

Her first reaction to seeing Ryan had been thinking that she had to resign and find another police department in another city. But then she'd thought, why should she? *He* had been the one who had behaved badly. *He* had been the one to break *her* heart, not the other way around. If anyone should have resigned and gone to another city, it was him.

But it had been plain that with his family embedded just outside of Tulsa, at the Lucky C ranch, Ryan wasn't going anywhere.

Well, neither was she.

At least, not anytime in the near future. She'd built up a good reputation here, not to mention a good rapport with the members of the police force, as well as the other people in the lab. Besides, her family lived in Tulsa. If she had left at that point, she would have felt that Ryan had pushed her out.

That was when she had made up her mind. She decided to dig in because she was *not* about to go anywhere. This was her home and she was staying. Ryan couldn't chase her away.

Since then, when their paths did cross, they had been polite but distant. He asked her no questions and she didn't interact with him at all. If any of his cases needed forensic backup, there were others in her lab she could refer the work to—which was exactly what she had done.

Until this latest incident involving vandalism and who knew what else on his family's ranch.

She knew in her heart—the same organ the man had so cavalierly dragged nails over—that she should be as professionally detached from this case as she might have been with any other case that crossed her desk. But, like it or not, the look in Ryan's eyes had gotten to her. He would have been surprised to know that beneath his carefully maintained, steely exterior, she saw the concern, the worry that was in his eyes.

For him, this was not just close to home, this *was* home, and he needed someone to help him navigate through the troubled waters until the culprit—whoever that turned out to be—was caught.

"That doesn't have to be you," Harold had glibly pointed out when she'd made her decision to lead the forensic investigation known to him. In the young intern's typically uncanny manner, he'd obviously honed in on her unspoken reasons for being at the crime scene. "We're actually competent enough to report back to you with the evidence. No need for you to come with us and hover around where Mr. Terrific can see you."

Where the lab intern got his flippant references from was beyond her, but she wasn't about to hang back and be perceived as having gone into hiding. She *knew* that was the way it would look to anyone who was aware of their—hers and Ryan's—history. Since Harold knew about them, she had little doubt that slowly but surely—or maybe even quickly— everyone else would know, as well.

It had become evident to her in lightning fashion, after the intern had been on the job for less than a few weeks, that he was nothing if not loyal to her. But Harold clearly also loved to talk, and inevitably everything he knew rose to the surface and burst out into the air with enthusiasm, like homing pigeons that had been locked up far too long when their cage door was accidentally opened.

So she told herself that she did it to keep her reputation as the head of the forensic lab intact, even though she was well aware that it was because she felt that Ryan—whether he knew it or not—needed someone in his corner. A sympathetic someone rather than someone looking to take him down a peg. Ryan was a good detective, but he was definitely not a beloved fixture around the precinct. He had a ways to go before his people skills rose above the level of "barely acceptable."

Which was why, whether he knew it or not, Ryan needed her. She just wasn't going to say as much out loud.

Ryan was more than a little surprised to see Susie getting out of the crime scene investigations SUV ahead of her forensic team. He'd put the call in to her, but he'd just assumed that, given their history, she would send her people without venturing out herself.

He was well aware that she was busy enough at the lab. This case had become a top priority to him, but it couldn't be the same for her. Her lab processed *all* the evidence that was taken in from the cases that were being handled by the department. That meant, as far as he could see, that one case for her was pretty much like another.

He didn't realize how happy he'd be to see her here until he was actually *looking* at her exit the SUV, carrying her forensic case in her hand.

He also had no idea that his mouth had dropped open as he watched her get out of the vehicle.

"If you don't close your mouth, if it starts raining like they said it might, you're liable to drown," Susie told him glibly as she walked right past him.

Confused, for a second he didn't know what Susie was talking about. And then, almost as an afterthought, he shut his mouth.

At least for a second.

And then he said, "I just didn't expect to see you here."

"Why? That was you on the phone, wasn't it?" she asked as if she wasn't acutely aware of the sound of his voice, a voice that for the first year after they broke up had haunted her every dream, her every thought. "Asking me to come out to the bunkhouse on the Lucky C," she said by way of a reminder.

Ryan shrugged, as if his call to her had been a mere formality. "Yes, but I was asking for your team to come out. I didn't think you'd come with them."

Susie paused and gave him a look he couldn't read. "Surprise," she declared flippantly. "Now, why don't you take me to the crime scene so the team and I can get down to work?" she suggested, deliberately sounding professional and removed.

It pleased her to see that just for a fraction of a moment, Ryan appeared the tiniest bit rattled by her presence.

"Sure," he said the next moment, pulling himself together. "Right in here." With that, he proceeded to lead the way to the bunkhouse.

His stride was longer and she had to lengthen hers, almost beginning to trot in order to keep up. She did rather than asking him to slow down.

"What can you tell me about the victim?" she asked.

Ryan didn't answer her immediately. They had reached the bunkhouse and he held the door open for her, letting her walk inside first.

Susie could see the dead man. The victim was lying on his back, staring unseeingly at the ceiling, a darkened pool of blood beneath him.

"He's twenty-four and was a relatively new hire on the ranch." Ryan said, answering her question.

"Twenty-four?" she repeated. A note of sorrow had entered her voice. "He's just a baby."

Ryan slanted a glance in her direction. "Said the old woman of thirty," he commented.

"Some of us *are* old at thirty," she pointed out with conviction. Heaven knew there were times she felt old, as if she had lived an entire lifetime already. Susie didn't bother looking in his direction to underscore her comment to him. Instead, she got down to business. "Do you know if he got into fights, had any enemies, got drunk and abusive on a regular basis?" she asked Ryan as she bent over the body for a closer look.

"All good questions," Ryan told her—she had no idea if he was being sarcastic or not—but then he answered, "No, no and no."

Well, that was no help, she thought, looking around. She tried not to move the body in any manner until the coroner arrived and had his time with the victim, taking whatever readings he needed to.

The man should have been here by now.

Turning to Ryan, she asked, "Has the coroner arrived yet?"

"Also no," Ryan told her. "But he's on his way. Or at least that was what he said when I called his office after I made the call to you."

She nodded. For now, she had to be satisfied taking photographs of the crime scene—and the victim—keeping a closer examination on ice until the coroner completed his on-site examination.

"I'm surprised Benson's letting you work this case, given your connection," Susie commented in between taking photographs of the scene from every angle.

Ryan avoided making eye contact with her. Instead, he shrugged and brazened it out. "I'm a good cop and the department's shorthanded."

"The department's always shorthanded, it's a given." And then Susie paused. Her eyes narrowed as she looked up at Ryan, scrutinizing him for a moment. "You didn't tell him about this, did you?"

For a brief second, Ryan thought about saying that of course he had. But for the most part, he relied on omissions to give the illusion that he was telling the truth. He didn't lie outright and decided that now was not the time to start. Especially since, for whatever reason, she had come out to help him.

"Not yet," he admitted. "I haven't gotten around to it."

"Uh-huh." She went back to taking photographs. Ryan didn't fool her for a moment. He hadn't called the chief, because he wanted to work the case. If Benson vetoed the idea, then he would be forced to stop. But if he didn't ask, then Benson couldn't say no. "And just when do you think you'll 'get around to it'?"

Ryan shrugged again as he followed her without realizing it. "Depends. How long before you can give me some input on time of death, cause of death—other than that the man bled out," he specified. "And any other useful, pertinent information?" he asked.

Finished with taking photographs for the time being, Susie set down her camera. "I can give you the 'any other useful, pertinent information' right now," she told him. "Go tell Benson," she instructed in a forceful, no-nonsense voice as she slipped on a pair of plastic gloves in order to conduct another phase of her examination.

But Ryan shook his head. "I'm too busy now," he told her.

She looked at him over her shoulder. "Too busy doing what?" she asked.

"Watching you and learning," Ryan replied, his face a mask of seriousness.

She had to stop what she was doing and give the

man his due. "You know, you keep a straight enough face, you could almost sell that."

Ryan inclined his head. For just the smallest island of time he allowed the years to dial back, and they were just two young people, hopelessly in love, with the world at their feet and endless possibilities in the wind. Back then he had almost convinced himself that scenario could last—and then the call had come, telling him his unit had been called up and he was to head back to the frontline fighting.

Then the possibilities disappeared like soap bubbles that couldn't live beyond the moment. The breakup, in his eyes, had been inevitable.

"I'll work on it," he told her, the coolness in his voice utterly dismissing her comment. "Now, how can I help?"

Most detectives didn't phrase things that way. They made it known that she was working "their" crime scenes and she was just a visitor while they were the major players—the ones who counted.

Susie couldn't help wondering if he had just made the offer to help to get on her good side. Most likely he had. It would be in keeping with the man she had come to know, not the one she had initially fallen in love with. In all likelihood, that man hadn't existed except in the recesses of her romantic soul.

Remember what he did to you. You didn't have any warning of that breakup coming, either. Don't buy into his charm or any other part of his act. You're older and supposedly wiser now. Don't play into his hand.

The silent pep talk wasn't working.

"You can stop hovering over me like that."

Susie raised her eyes to his. Damn but she had loved his eyes. They were so green, they reminded her of the ocean, an ocean she had wanted to go wading in. To get lost in.

Now the only part of that that had been prophetic was the word *lost*.

"I don't do well with hovering," she informed him coolly.

Ryan raised his hands as if surrendering to her instructions. "Backing up now," he informed her. "No longer hovering."

"Since you're no longer hovering, you could try calling Benson and letting him know we're working a homicide that happened on your family's ranch. If the chief finds out from someone else, it's not going to be pretty—and it won't go well for you," she warned Ryan. "He doesn't like not being on top of things—or at least in the loop to start with."

Ryan knew she was right.

However, that didn't make the chore ahead of him any more palatable. The second he told his superior the location where the homicide had taken place, there was a strong chance he would be taken off the case. He could operate in so-called ignorance for only so long. If he was told to get off the case, he would have to follow orders.

What he needed to do was frame his argument for staying before he actually called the less-than-friendly chief of police with an update.

He supposed if the chief took him off the case, he could always put in for some vacation time and take on the investigation privately.

Ryan felt that his father would respond a great deal better to having a member of the family questioning him rather than a stranger. When it came to Big J, he knew just how to phrase things in order to not get his father's back up. A great deal of time could be wasted that way, apologizing for inferring the wrong thing or saying something that his father perceived to be an insult to him or to his family— or worse, to both.

Ryan heard the phone on the other end being picked up. "Chief, it's Colton. Just hear me out on this before you make up your mind how you want to go ahead on this case."

"What case?" Benson asked gruffly, suspicion weaving itself through his words.

Definitely not friendly and open to suspending a few rules, Ryan thought. "There's a dead ranch hand at the Lucky C."

"Regular fun house, that ranch of yours," he heard Benson mutter.

The chief was being cryptic, but for the life of him, Ryan had no idea how to take the man's comment.

Chapter 6

Hoping for the best, Ryan plowed ahead, giving the chief all the details that he had available to him at the present time.

However, at least for now, he left out the fact that, according to the tests that had previously been run, forensics had placed his sister at the scene of the last act of vandalism on the ranch. Ryan placated his conscience by telling himself that for the time being, Benson didn't need that particular piece of information regarding a minor crime cluttering up the details that surrounded this latest, far more serious occurrence at the Lucky C.

When Ryan was finished relaying what he knew, he paused, waiting for his superior's input.

The chief made him wait for a while, or at least it felt that way to Ryan. When the chief did finally speak, it was to ask him another question. "That's all you've got?"

Ryan curbed his impatience. He wanted nothing more than to be done with this unproductive back-and-forth exchange.

"So far, yes. The coroner's on his way and the CSI unit just arrived a few minutes ago," he replied, measuring out each word as he waited for the chief's final verdict.

When none was volunteered, Ryan pushed the matter a little further, thinking that maybe a direct approach was necessary. "So, can I continue working the investigation?"

There was another prolonged pause before he heard the chief say, "You're right, you know."

At this point, Ryan felt as if he was in some sort of strange game of hide-and-seek—and he, apparently, was "it." What was "hiding" was the one word he was waiting to hear: *yes*.

"About?" Ryan asked, doing his best to sound as if he was relaxed instead of edgy. It was bad enough that this was happening on what was essentially his home turf. To be kept dangling on the outskirts like this was almost more than he could put up with.

"Under normal circumstances, I'd tell you to get your tail out of there pronto and hand off the case to someone else. Except that right now there *is* no some-one else. But you already knew that, didn't you?"

He could almost feel Benson's dark eyes drilling into him. Ryan knew better than to feign ignorance around the chief. Chief Benson had been around the block more than once and seemed to be uncannily up on almost everything that was going on in his territory—and if he wasn't, he would be before the day was out.

So Ryan said, "Yes, sir," in a genial voice and waited for the chief's orders.

"So you already know," Benson bit off, "that you'll be working the case until Detective Mahoney comes off sick leave and we get people to fill those other two vacancies in Homicide that I suddenly, for no apparent reason, find myself staring at."

Ryan had been well aware that two detectives in his department had put in their papers, one for re-tirement and one for transfer to a different depart-ment. Benson wasn't everyone's cup of tea. "Just wanted to make sure, sir," Ryan responded and felt safe in magnanimously adding, "I don't like taking anything for granted."

He heard Benson make some sort of unintelligible noise that might or might not have been a grunt, or possibly a disparaging remark about the "humble" card he'd just played.

Ryan braced himself to be chewed out—the chief

was an expert at it—but instead, what he heard from his superior was, "Keep me posted, Colton."

The next second, the chief abruptly hung up before another word could be exchanged.

Just as well, Ryan thought.

Ryan wasn't aware of blowing out a long, relieved breath as he closed his cell phone and pocketed it again, but Susie was.

She had edged nearer ever so slightly and had been quietly watching Ryan beneath hooded eyes as he made the call to the chief of police. She felt fairly confident that no one else noticed her observing the detective even as she went about her work, carefully documenting everything in its place before taking samples with what appeared to a layman to be an elongated version of a Q-tip that was then deposited into a long, see-through, cylindrical tube with a cap on top to keep it in place.

When Ryan turned in her direction, she could see by his expression that he was suddenly aware of the fact that she'd overheard his conversation.

She tried to make light of it. "I take it you managed to sweet-talk the chief into letting you stay on the case?"

Somewhat preoccupied, Ryan was momentarily confused by her statement. "What?"

Susie waved her words away. They certainly didn't bear repeating. "Just kidding," she told him.

"Besides, we both know that you're not physically capable of sweet talk."

At that point Ryan had replayed her words in his head. "It's not necessary to sweet-talk the chief into letting me work the case when the department's shorthanded."

"Lucky you," she replied glibly.

She meant something by that, he thought. Most likely it was some sort of hidden reference to their time together—or, more specifically, to the breakup. But he didn't have time to get into that now, or to feel guilty for the way he had treated her. Definitely not his finest hour, but he'd had his reasons.

He changed the subject. "How long is it going to take you to process all this?" he asked, waving his hand around to indicate the new crime scene.

She didn't even pause to calculate a ballpark figure. "That all depends on whether you want a rush job or a thorough job."

Ryan frowned. He didn't want the former, but the latter implied a long wait. "Can't it be both?" he asked.

She knew he was going to ask something like that. Susie sighed. "We'll do our best," she told him, speaking for her team.

At least she was being honest—and she wasn't playing up her part in this or the fact that some considered forensics more important than the department's actual legwork. She was, if nothing else, a team player. He just had to get used to the idea that they were part of the same team.

Ryan inclined his head. "Can't ask for more than that."

The comment—the last word in reasonableness—surprised her, and she looked at Ryan. "Oh, you can ask," she told him.

He knew what that meant. He could ask until he was blue in the face, but she was only going to deliver what she could. That was all right by him.

"Have someone come get me once the coroner gets here and finishes his preliminary exam," Ryan requested just before he started to walk out of the bunkhouse.

Susie snapped her fingers, as if suddenly remembering something. "Drat, I'm afraid I left all my lackeys at the lab," she told him glibly, indicating that she had no one to send to him with the message.

Ryan's mouth curved ever so slightly, a hint of a smile in his eyes. "You'll find a way," he countered confidently. "You always do."

With that, he went out to the corral. He knew from experience that the other ranch hands had gathered there to exchange information and theories—and speculate on all sorts of things that were related to the murder of the newest hire at the ranch. Back in the day, the same corral had been a favorite gathering spot for him and his siblings.

Drawing closer to the corral, Ryan smiled to

himself. He was right. There were six ranch hands presently in the corral. None of them were even pretending to be doing anything remotely connected to their work. Instead, they were all over to one side, conferring. They appeared uneasy.

More so when they saw him approaching.

Ryan noticed Juan Alvarez nudging the man next to him and nodding in his direction as he came up to the gathering.

An uneasy silence wiggled its way into and through the group.

Not exactly the most comfortable of situations, Ryan thought to himself. But then, he hadn't gone into law enforcement for the comfort of the work. He'd gone into it to keep the peace and to make sure that the good people were safe by rounding up the bad ones and separating them from the general population.

"Anything any of you boys can tell me about Kurt Rodgers?" Ryan asked as he leaned against the corral and looked from one ranch hand to the next.

The ranch hands shrugged, almost in unison. After a beat, a cacophony of mumbled negative responses met his question.

"Nothing?" Ryan questioned in surprise, his piercing gaze shifting from one face to another. "C'mon, you guys must have some kind of an opinion about the man. What did he do in his down time? Did he drink too much? Gamble to excess? Get on somebody's bad side?" He looked from one face to the next as he threw out possible vices and offenses. None of the men's expressions changed or gave anything away. "Nothing?" he questioned skeptically. "What was Rodgers, a saint?"

"He kept to himself mostly," a wiry, redheaded ranch hand appropriately nicknamed "Red" said.

The others instantly bobbed their heads up and down in agreement.

"Best one to ask about Rodgers is Miss Greta," another ranch hand—Jim Walsh—volunteered.

Ryan turned his attention to Walsh. Why he cringed inwardly when his sister's name was brought up he didn't want to think about. It wasn't something he could have easily explained if Benson were here. Luckily, the man wasn't, and besides, he hadn't cringed outwardly, which was all that really mattered.

He did his best to sound casual as he asked Walsh, "Why Greta?"

"'Cause Rodgers was working with her, helping her train the horses. I heard her telling him that he had a real knack for it. Rodgers lit up like a damn Christmas tree every time she said a kind word to him," Walsh recalled. There was nothing in his voice to indicate that he was jealous of the man or the attention Rodgers had garnered from Greta.

"Well, he ain't gonna be lighting up no more," another one of the hands declared dourly.

"Somebody should go and tell her what happened," another of the ranch hands, George O'Brien, said, looking at Ryan. "She's gonna be real upset about losing him."

Walsh made a dismissive noise and Ryan looked in his direction, waiting for more. He didn't have that long to wait.

"She didn't look like she was worried about losing him yesterday. I heard her yelling something at Rodgers and he looked real upset," Walsh told the others. "And confused as hell to boot."

"Wait a second," Ryan said, interrupting Walsh before the latter could veer off topic. None of what the ranch hand said made any sense to him. "You saw my sister here yesterday?"

"Yes, sir," Walsh answered respectfully. "And she looked pretty mad, too. And Rodgers, he seemed like he was scared and confused at the same time. I just thought it was 'cause he'd done something wrong with the horses. I've never heard Miss Greta yelling like that before," he admitted. "Hell, if you don't mind my saying so, I've never heard her yelling before."

"Me, neither," Alvarez agreed.

Ryan had, but only when she was greatly provoked—and he'd never heard of her yelling at the people who worked for them. She wasn't one who liked throwing her weight around and thought little of people who did.

Setting that aside, Ryan went on questioning Walsh. He wasn't through with the ranch hand yet.

"You actually *saw* my sister here yesterday?" he asked the older ranch hand.

Ryan moved so that he was rather close to being in the man's face. He did it in order to cut Walsh off from the other men in the corral. In these sorts of situations, he'd learned that the person being questioned looked to take his cue from the friends—or at the very least, the people—standing around him.

Almost reluctantly, Walsh nodded his head. "Yes, sir, I did."

Ryan had a sinking feeling in the pit of his stomach. When he'd spoken to her, Greta had sworn she was in Oklahoma City and had been there for three weeks now. "You're absolutely sure of that," Ryan pressed.

Walsh straightened slightly, bringing his shoulders back like a soldier, not like a career ranch hand. "Yes, sir, I am," he said solemnly.

Ryan approached the statement from every side he could, never taking his eyes off the ranch hand. "You saw her here, on the Lucky C."

"If you don't want me to say that, then I won't," Walsh volunteered.

"What I want is for you to tell me the truth, never mind what I'd like to hear," Ryan told him sternly.

The cowhand bobbed his head up and down with feeling. "Then yes, sir, I saw her. Miss Greta, she was here, at the ranch." He paused for a split second, as if debating his next words. And then he said, "I thought there might have been something, well, wrong."

There *was* something wrong, Ryan thought. But what? Was there something about his sister that he wasn't aware of? Or was there someone in the vicinity that just *looked* like Greta? That would explain some of it, but not everything. It certainly didn't explain the DNA findings that Susie had documented.

"Why's that?" he asked Walsh.

Walsh was visibly uncomfortable saying this, Ryan noted. "There was this really weird look on Miss Greta's face, like, I dunno, she was listening to someone give her orders, some inner voice or something like that," he added, shrugging his shoulders.

This was beginning to sound stranger and stranger. *Was* Greta having a breakdown? Or was there some sort of other explanation? In either case, Ryan was instantly even more alert than he had been a few minutes ago.

"Go on," he ordered sternly.

Walsh shrugged helplessly, obviously looking for a way to explain what he meant. "She had this expression on her face—like she'd sucked on a bunch of lemons and she was mad at the world because of it."

Ryan nodded, then glanced at the other ranch hands again. "Anyone else see my sister here yesterday? Or hear her having words with Rodgers?" He looked from one face to another. "Anything?" he pressed, unsure if he actually *wanted* to hear anything more or not. But he was a cop—it was his job to get to the bottom of things, not just the neat and tidy cases, but *all* of them.

A disjoined gaggle of heads, all shaking at their own tempo, told Ryan that was all the confirmation—and information—regarding the murder that he was going to get from this group. If anyone else *had* witnessed Greta saying or doing something yesterday, they were keeping it to themselves.

"Thanks, that's all for now," he said to the ranch hands. "I'll get back to you."

Dismissed, the group wasted no time in quickly dispersing.

Feeling drained, Ryan turned and saw his father walking toward him slowly. Each step for the man was obviously an effort.

It almost hurt to see the once robust man in this condition. Ryan wished his father would stay put and rest more. He was no doctor, but he knew that getting tired certainly didn't help his father's condition any.

Striding toward the older man quickly, Ryan deliberately cut his father's "journey" short. He wasn't looking forward to this part, either, but he needed to confront his father on this overlooked piece of information.

"You didn't tell me that Greta was here yesterday, Dad."

Big J looked at his son as if he had caught his

third born in a lie. For the sake of argument, John Colton allowed that what Ryan was alleging was actually true.

"That's 'cause I didn't know," Big J told him. "You sure about this information, boy?" his father asked. "She usually comes by the house when she's here, you know, to talk with her mama and maybe spend a little time with her—and with her old man." Big J rolled the question put to him over in his head a second time. Frowning slightly, the patriarch was forced to shake his head. "I think someone's pulling your leg, boy. Greta wasn't here yesterday. I'd bet you a big steak dinner at the best restaurant in Tulsa that she wasn't. She ain't been here for more than three weeks, as I recall."

He paused again, thinking. Ryan didn't rush him, but waited for his father to speak again.

"She's off down in Oklahoma City," his father declared, happy that he remembered. "That's where she spends most of her time these days, being around that man she claims to be so in love with."

Ryan could tell by his father's expression that although the match was seen as a prestigious one in general, Big J didn't think that his daughter's fiancé was good enough for her.

The mantra of every father since Adam, Ryan couldn't help thinking.

His father's next words confirmed it. "You ask me, he don't deserve her, but then," he concluded with a shrug, "nobody's asking me, so I'm keeping my mouth shut."

That would be the day, Ryan thought. His father *never* kept his opinions to himself. Everyone and his brother knew if the big man was displeased or if someone or something had rubbed him the wrong way. Everyone was well aware of the fact that his father was *not* a man given to suffering in silence.

Getting back to the matter at hand, Ryan thought his father sounded very adamant about Greta not having been here at the ranch recently.

Just as convinced as Walsh had been that Greta *was* here.

They couldn't both be right.

Either his father really hadn't seen Greta—or he had, and for some reason he was being protective of her. It wasn't impossible. After all, she was the youngest and a girl to boot. His father often protected the "weakling," although Greta would probably really balk at that description. It didn't fit her. As far as he and his brothers were concerned, their baby sister was a scrapper.

Walsh's scenario was still believable—except he still couldn't come up with a reason why Greta would go off on someone she worked with that way. She just wasn't the type to throw her weight—or the fact that she was a Colton—around. It wasn't in her nature.

Actually, from everything he had ever witnessed, Greta's behavior was quite the opposite. She loved working with horses, loved being a mentor to anyone else who shared the same passion.

The more he found out about this case, the less he felt he knew.

He sincerely hoped that Susie could come up with something after she and her team gathered up all the pertinent traces they needed to analyze, because apparently forensic evidence was all he was going to be able to trust.

Even if he wasn't quite willing to admit that to Susie yet.

Chapter 7

Walking back to the bunkhouse, Ryan was just in time to see the coroner's vehicle disappearing from view, obviously on its way back to the coroner's office.

His mood was none too cheerful when he walked into what was still an active crime scene.

Susie was just wrapping up her initial investigation and repacking her case. He lost no time in getting over to her. "You were supposed to have someone come get me when Doc got here," he reminded her, irritated over the lost opportunity.

Susie looked up and just for a moment, she found herself distracted. Maybe it was the expression on his face, or the sound of his voice, but she had to struggle to keep her mind from wandering back to another, better time. She was going to have to watch that, she silently lectured. If she slipped up, there would be questions about her competence.

Shaking off her thoughts, she braced herself for a display of temper.

"No," she corrected, "you said you wanted to talk to him when he finished his preliminary examination. But the second he was done, Doc started packing up to leave. I tried to tell him to wait because you wanted to talk to him." She paused, not for effect, but to get the wording just right. "I believe his exact words were 'If he wants to talk to me, he can come to the coroner's office. Colton knows where it is.'"

Ryan shook his head. "The man gets more cantankerous every day," he complained.

Susie went back to packing up. "Well, in Doc's defense, being a coroner isn't exactly a fun line of work."

The way he saw it, that was no excuse. "Yeah, but the man knew that when he signed up for it," Ryan pointed out.

Susie's eyes narrowed as she took a closer look at the man in front of her. Funny how she'd gotten to be so good at reading someone she kept trying to convince herself she didn't care about any longer. She supposed it was like riding a bicycle. Once you learned how, you never really lost the knack.

"Ryan, what's wrong?" she asked.

Ryan.

He felt something stir inside. She hadn't called him by his first name since before he had deployed to the Middle East all those many years ago. More than an eternity ago. When they ran into one another that first time after their breakup, she hadn't really called him anything—which he felt was a better way to go, seeing as how if she had called him something, he had a feeling it wouldn't have been anything that was repeatable in polite society.

Whenever she'd been forced to address him since then, she'd used either his last name or his rank, never his first name.

That she called him by his given name now changed the parameters a bit for him. He wasn't altogether sure what to make of it yet, or how he felt about it.

The real problem was, he didn't want to *feel* at all.

"What do you mean?" he asked, stalling.

"I mean you look like you just found out you're going to have to go on a fifty-mile forced march through the desert with a seventy-five-pound backpack strapped to your back—after having run a marathon. So talk. What's wrong?" she repeated just a tad more forcefully.

He debated whether or not to let her know, then decided that she'd undoubtedly find out, one way or another. She was dogged that way.

"One of the ranch hands said he overheard Greta arguing with our victim yesterday."

"Yesterday?" Susie echoed. Her eyebrows drew together as confusion had her narrowing her eyes. "Didn't you tell me that your sister wasn't in Tulsa yesterday?"

Just talking about it—and the idea that Greta might have lied to him—really annoyed Ryan. When he answered, he sounded almost waspish. "Yeah, that's what I told you because that's what she told me when I called and talked to her."

"The ranch hand could have been mistaken," she told Ryan, giving him a way out. "Did you ask your father about that?"

"Yes." Ryan all but bit off the single word.

Getting information out of Ryan was like pulling teeth. It just wasn't in the man's nature to be forthcoming. "What did he say?" Susie pressed.

Ryan sighed and repeated in a monotone, "That she couldn't have been here because she would have stopped by to see my mother and him the way she always does when she's back in Tulsa. Hell, she stays at the house each and every time."

It wasn't hard to read between the lines. "But you don't believe him," she concluded.

Ryan shrugged almost helplessly. "Big J would cover for Greta if he had to. And who knows, maybe she doesn't come by to see my parents each time she's in town. Maybe there was some other reason that Greta was here and she didn't want anyone else to know about it." He looked at Susie and his frown deepened measurably. "I know what you're thinking."

"You've added mind reading to your repertoire," she pretended to marvel, duly "impressed."

"That must come in handy, given your line of work," she said.

"Don't get smart with me, Howard," Ryan warned, deliberately using her last name to keep a professional distance between them no matter how much he wanted to bring this to a personal level. He told himself that he was dealing with too much at the moment to cope with that added dimension—a dimension he recalled vividly no matter what he told himself to the contrary.

The more time he spent around Susie, the more those memories from the past tried to claim him.

Susan assumed an innocent expression. "But I thought that the department liked their forensic experts to be smart."

Ryan shot her a dark look. His temper was dangerously close to the surface. It was a vain attempt to stop his feelings from getting the better of him. "You know what I mean."

"Not usually," she admitted. "But according to that comment of yours, you seem to think that you know what I mean—or at least what I'm thinking."

"You were thinking that there was no point in

me going back and forth about whether or not Greta was here since you already had her DNA placing her at the last so-called crime scene. And if she was at one, why wouldn't she be at this latest one? Well, I can tell you why—because there's a big difference between breaking a window and leaving graffiti on the wall, and killing someone."

"No one's arguing that point," Susie pointed out. "Least of all me."

Finished packing, Susie closed the lid on her case and snapped the locks into place. The black valise was completely filled with vials and tiny containers, each with separate samples of possible evidence that might, with any luck, just lead them to the identity of Kurt Rodgers's killer.

Susie patted the closed case. "Well, I've got my work cut out for me, so I'm going to get my team together and go back to the lab to see what we can find out."

She was about to walk away from him when she stopped abruptly and turned around to look at Ryan again. She knew she was going to regret this. After all this time, her heart should have hardened to at least flint grade, if not downright steel.

But the look she saw in his eyes had gotten to her. There was something about Ryan Colton that *always* got to her, despite all her concerted efforts to keep her distance and notwithstanding all the internal pep talks she gave herself.

The bottom line was that she just couldn't stand to see him in pain.

"You had lunch yet?" she asked.

Ryan stared at the woman he had once cut loose for the noblest of reasons as if she had just launched into some strange, alien tongue.

But then he made sense of her words. Thinking for a moment, he tried to remember what his morning had been like before he'd gotten the call that brought him here. He shook his head.

"No, I don't think I even had breakfast yet." At least none that he could remember. "Definitely not lunch."

"Neither have I," she told him matter-of-factly. "I work better with something in my stomach. You want to stop and grab a cup of coffee and a couple of sandwiches or something?" she suggested.

The offer to in essence go out for lunch together caught him completely off guard. "You mean to go?"

Susie shrugged, indifferent to the choice. "To go, to stay, whatever. Just something to sustain us and remind us that we're still human and not just robots engaged in endlessly processing crime scenes."

There, she thought, that put it all in vague enough terms. She figured that would make it harder for him to find a reason to pass up the suggestion.

Ryan thought her offer over for a minute. "I still have to talk to the coroner."

"Doc's on his way to the office and he's not going

anywhere—unless there's another dead body to pick up," she qualified, "which I hope to God there isn't."

Ryan had to admit that she had a point. He knew from experience that he didn't do all that well running on empty and coffee always helped to jump-start his brain. Pocketing the badly worn notepad he used to collect stray data and even more stray thoughts, Ryan crossed over to Susie.

Acting on manners that had been bred into him so that his reaction was automatic, he took her case from her, intent on carrying it to the car.

The second the case changed hands, it commandeered all of his attention. "Wow, you didn't tell me the coroner's having you transport the body in your case. This is *heavy*," he declared. Ryan looked at the five-foot-seven woman with new respect. "You carry this case yourself?"

She flashed a quick smile in his direction, reacting to the question, not the man. "Like I said, my lackeys are at the office." And then she became serious. "Of course I carry that myself."

His eyes slid over her from top to bottom. She was curvy but not particularly strong-looking. He would have expected her to struggle with this sort of weight. And yet, she had easily moved the heavy case.

The woman had to be all muscle, he couldn't help thinking. Either that, or just too damn stubborn to ask anyone for help. He had a feeling it was at least partially the latter. "You know, you're a lot stronger than you look," he said as he accompanied her to her vehicle.

Opening the truck, her eyes met his. "I have to be," she replied.

Susie banked down the urge to say something more. Instead, she got in behind the steering wheel and buckled up, waiting for Ryan to do the same in the shotgun seat. Once he did, she took off.

She didn't have to say more. The message still came across. It always did—frequently—courtesy of his guilty conscience. A conscience that never allowed him to forget for long how she must have felt when he forced himself to cut her loose, letting her know not in person, or even over the phone, but via a letter with half a world between them.

That made up his mind for him. "I guess the evidence isn't going to go anywhere if I take forty minutes for lunch."

"Good response, especially considering that you're already in my car and I'm driving," Susie said with a laugh.

He'd always loved the sound of that laugh and tried not to allow it to filter through him. "Do you have any place in particular in mind?"

"Any place they have food is fine with me," she told him. "I'm not picky."

The corners of his mouth lifted. Memories flooded his brain, even though he had made no effort to summon them. "Yeah, I remember that about you."

Susie inclined her head. "I'm flattered you remember something."

Ryan didn't know if she was being serious, or just flippant. He certainly couldn't blame her if it was the latter.

"I remember a lot," he asserted quietly.

It took a moment for her to respond. "Must come in handy when you're working a case."

Was she putting him in his place, or reminding him that they were professionals and that despite the fact that they were stopping to eat, it was just in the framework of being two coworkers and nothing more?

Regardless of her intent, it was safer for him to go with the latter scenario. But at this point in his life, did he really *want* to be all that safe?

Safe was synonymous with isolated, with cut off. With being alone. And he'd been that way—alone in the only way that it mattered—for a long, long time. Maybe what he really needed was a change.

Leopards don't change their spots.

It was a hackneyed saying at best, but he couldn't help thinking it still contained more than an element of truth in it.

Maybe he *couldn't* change, not at this stage of his life.

Susie glanced at him as she took a corner, turning down a one-way street.

"You know, it's all right to talk," she told him.

"I'm taking us to get something to eat, not picking up a quart of hemlock to sneak into your drinking water. You don't have to sit there like you're facing death."

He supposed she was right. He was overthinking this and taking it far too seriously. It was lunch— food—not a commitment for life.

With a shrug, he gave her a vague excuse. "I was just thinking."

She accepted the excuse and joked, "I thought I heard wheels grinding. Did you know that the best thing for your mind is to let it relax once in a while, have a little free-form fun?"

He knew she was kidding, but in reality, there was some truth to that school of thought. Still, he felt he couldn't concede that point to her without first delivering some sort of a comeback.

"I must have missed that in my latest copy of *Health and Welfare Guide*," he quipped.

"Well then, consider it my gift to you," Susie told him.

He didn't need another gift from her. The one she had given him ten years ago—when she'd given him herself—was more than he felt worthy of, especially given his subsequent behavior. The memory of their breakup made Ryan uncomfortable again. He shouldn't be here like this with her. The most innocent of things could easily become too tempting in a blink of an eye.

"Look, maybe this wasn't such a good idea," he

told her, beginning to beg off. "If you drop me back at my car, I'll just take a rain check—"

"Too late," she declared. "We're here. No need to talk about rain checks. It'll only take a few minutes. We'll get it to go," she proposed as a compromise— she would have preferred sitting at a booth in the restaurant, even if the restaurant *was* geared toward fast food.

"And then you can," she continued. "Go, I mean," she added in case she had lost him. He had a look on his face that she couldn't place. "We'll use the drive-through," Susie added as she steered her vehicle into the lane that fed past the outdoor menu and its companying speaker. "It'll be faster that way."

"Not usually," Ryan contradicted.

In his experience, unless it involved a fast-food run sometime in the dead of night, he'd found that using the drive-through window, rather than just going into the restaurant and ordering something to go, took more time. Cars would queue up behind one another, moving at what amounted to a snail's pace, especially at the window where they paid.

And inevitably, there would be one, at times two, drivers directly in front of his car who would have trouble making up their minds as to what they wanted to order.

"Trust me on this," Susie told him. They reached the order window rather quickly.

"Welcome to Burger Heaven. What can we serve you today?"

Ryan saw her smile widely in response to the server's voice. "This'll be quick," Susie promised him in a whisper before asking in an audible voice, "Rusty?"

"That you, Susie-Q?" the deep, hearty voice asked, clearly pleased to hear hers.

"One and the same," Susie answered. "I want the usual—except that I want two of them, packed in separate bags."

"You got it, Susie-Q. Two usuals. Go on through. They'll be waiting for you at window three."

Susie shifted her car into Drive and glided her vehicle around the corner of the building.

"What's a usual?" Ryan asked once they were moving again.

Rather than answering his question, Susie allowed a smile to play on her lips. "You'll see."

Driving through, Susie had her money—down to the exact penny—ready in her hand when it came her turn at the next window.

A tall, heavyset young man, who obviously enjoyed more than his share of complimentary meals at the fast-food restaurant, was waiting for them—or rather her—at the last window. He had two large bags in one hand and a sturdy cardboard tray holding two tall, covered soft drinks in the other.

As Susie snaked the CSI SUV up to the window,

the uniformed attendant leaned slightly forward to reach her. Susie offered him a wide smile as she took first the bags, then the tray, handing each over to Ryan in the passenger seat.

"Always a pleasure, Susie-Q," the young man said, beaming broadly.

Susie responded with warmth. "Same here, Rusty. Take care of yourself."

The attendant winked, obviously enjoying the short, carefree flirtation, or so it appeared from where Ryan was sitting. "I always do, Susie-Q. I always do."

"What was that all about?" Trying to balance the two bags and the tray with their soft drinks as he held them on his lap, Ryan asked the question the moment she drove away from the last window.

"Lunch." She glanced at him, amused, just before she left the parking lot and went back out onto the open road. "You sure you're really a detective?" she teased.

"Sometimes," he said, thinking back to the case waiting for him the second his lunch break was over, "I'm not all that sure."

What he was sure of was that right now he wanted to be anything *but* a detective. Especially if his sister wound up being implicated.

Or worse.

Chapter 8

"It's circumstantial, but it *is* there."

Susie hated having to tell him this almost as much, judging by the expression on his face, as Ryan hated hearing it. But she had no choice.

A full day had gone by and she'd run all the tests she could think of. The results were still the same. Another damning piece of the puzzle was coming together. Another piece that pointed to Ryan's sister being behind this latest, not to mention the most serious, crime to have occurred on the grounds of the Lucky C ranch.

Working feverishly for the past day, when these results came in, she had still been debating how to

break the news to Ryan when he had suddenly turned
up in her lab. Dispensing with any small talk or niceties, he had gone right to the heart of his reason
for being there: he asked if any headway had been
made with what she and her team had collected at
the bunkhouse.

Knowing that there was no getting around this,
Susie took him into her cubbyhole of an office so
that she could talk to him without anyone else over-
hearing. If nothing else, she felt she owed Ryan that
much. It was only common decency.

Approaching the subject slowly, she began by referring to the prints that had been lifted from on and
around the bunkhouse door. There had been myriad
prints, which had turned out to be matches for all of
the current hired hands who occupied the bunkhouse.

The only prints that hadn't belonged to any of the
other ranch hands had belonged to Greta.

Ryan's face darkened. He was not receiving the
news well. But for a moment, he said nothing.

Despite everything he had once put her through,
Susie's heart went out to him.

"You realize that there's any number of reasons
why Greta's prints would be on the door," Susie
pointed out. "After all, your sister *did* stay at the
ranch a great deal, and she *was* in charge of training
the horses. Since Rodgers was her assistant, they had
to have interacted, and that's all this might be." Susie
shrugged, as if what she was saying to him was self-

evident. "Greta could have innocently come by the bunkhouse, looking for Rodgers if he wasn't ready to work with the horses when she was."

"So now you're on her side?" Ryan demanded sharply, his voice echoing with the stress he was laboring under. This latest piece of information piled on the already damning stack of evidence against Greta was almost too much for him to deal with.

The next moment, Ryan flushed, regretting his momentary lapse. He had no right to take his frustration with the investigation out on Susie. She was just doing her job, something he would have to do even though his family was going to be dead set against his doing it.

An apology rose to his lips, but Susie didn't give him a chance to say it.

"I don't take sides, Colton," Susie retorted in the same sharp tone that he had used. "I interpret the evidence." And then her voice softened just a touch. "Look, you know your sister a lot better than I do. Be honest now, do you think that Greta is capable of actually killing someone?"

"*Everyone's* capable of killing someone if they're pushed hard enough," Ryan answered her none too happily. It was a hard fact of life, but he had seen it happen before.

Susie appeared uncomfortable with his answer. "That's really cold." Her eyes narrowed, scrutinizing Ryan. "Is that what you really believe?"

Ryan sighed. He looked almost worn to her. "I don't know what I believe anymore. But I do know that I've got enough on Greta to bring her in for questioning. Maybe even arrest her," he added quietly, hating the very sound of the words, hating being put in this position.

Susie upbraided herself for being an idiot, but she still felt sorry for him, for what he had to be going through. And she said as much.

"Oh, Ryan, I'm so sorry."

Ryan's laugh was harsh and completely devoid of even a single drop of humor. "You and me both, Susie." And then, as if he had come to some sort of an internal conclusion, Ryan squared his shoulders, as if bracing himself for what he was going to be forced to have to do. "If you find anything else with those fancy whirling machines of yours—" he waved his hand vaguely behind him at the lab equipment that was right outside her tiny office "—call me and let me know."

Not waiting for her to make any sort of a response, Ryan walked out.

Susie rose and stood in the doorway of her office, looking after Ryan for a long moment, fighting the urge to run after him, to offer to help him bear the load before it broke him.

But she knew better than that. Ryan was much too proud to accept any help. He was infuriatingly stubborn that way.

And maybe, just maybe, that had been what had made her fall in love with him in the first place.

With a deep sigh, Susie left her tiny office and went back into the lab.

She had work to do.

"Are you crazy?" Jack demanded angrily a little more than an hour later.

Ryan had come to him, looking for Greta and asking if she was there at the old main house. When his older brother had said no, of course not, Ryan had pressed the issue, wanting to know if he was hiding her because she'd asked him to.

Jack looked at him as if he had lost his mind. "Greta's not here. She's not even in Tulsa. Why would I be hiding her?" he demanded. "Why would she even *ask* me to hide her?"

It killed Ryan to even say this, but he wasn't here as one of the Colton brothers—he was here in his official capacity. "Because she killed Kurt Rodgers and needed a place to lie low for a while."

Jack stared at him as if he had just turned into a stranger right before his eyes. After a second, he shook his head.

"You *are* crazy," Jack declared, then demanded, "Do you even *hear* yourself? Greta killed Kurt Rodgers? Greta doesn't even kill *spiders*, for God sakes. She catches them and puts them outside, like some kind of patron saint of creepy-crawlies. Greta's our golden girl, not to mention that she's hip-deep in planning her wedding to that jerk, Mark. Killing Rodgers isn't on her to-do list," Jack angrily assured him. "Between the wedding and her work, Greta doesn't have time for any extracurricular activities like killing people."

Ryan struggled to keep his temper under control. "This isn't a joke, Jack."

"And I'm not joking," Jack retorted, raising his voice so that it would be heard over Ryan's. "Get this through your thick head. Greta didn't kill Rodgers, so pick up your marbles and go play somewhere else," he ordered.

Drawn by the sound of raised voices coming from the front room, Brett, Daniel and Eric came in to join in on the argument in progress. All three looked from one brother to the next.

As the next oldest, Eric spoke up first. "What's all the shouting about?"

"Nobody's shouting," Ryan bit off, all but growling the words.

The three latecomers exchanged looks. "There're some cracks in the ceiling that beg to differ with you," Brett told Ryan and Jack. "C'mon, guys, give. What's this all about?"

Ryan did *not* want to get into this with the others, but Jack spoke up.

Jerking his thumb at Ryan, he accused, "He thinks

Greta's behind all the weird stuff that's been happening here at the ranch."

Eric looked stunned. "You're not talking about killing Rodgers, are you?"

"Among other things, yeah, he is," Jack confirmed angrily, glaring at Ryan.

Brett joined in, as outraged as Jack and Eric were. "You're crazy, Ryan. This is *Greta*," he stressed. "She couldn't have killed Rodgers."

"That's what I told him," Jack said.

The look Jack gave Ryan put him on notice that the line had been drawn in the sand, and Ryan was standing on one side of it with his brothers all gathered on the other.

Eric turned to look closely at Ryan. "So just what is it that you intend to do?" he asked, crossing his arms before his chest and looking, for all the world, as if he was sitting in judgment of his younger brother's actions.

Damn it, didn't they realize that he hated this as much as they did? "I'm going to bring Greta down to the precinct for questioning," Ryan informed his brothers stoically.

"Like a common criminal?" Jack accused.

"Like a suspect," Ryan answered, holding his ground and hating that it had come to this. But if his brothers were going to bandy words around, they damn well better bandy the right ones. "Look, I don't want her to be guilty any more than you do, but I've got to work with the facts and the facts point to her being at the site of the break-in at the stables, and her prints *were* found on the bunkhouse door."

"Yeah, along with everybody else's prints. Dad's fingerprints are probably all over the bunkhouse. You want to bring him in for questioning to see if he killed Rodgers?" Eric asked heatedly.

"Leave Ryan alone," Daniel told his brothers. "He's just doing his job. It's hard enough for him as it is without all of you ganging up on him and giving him guff." He glanced in Ryan's direction, reading his half brother's weary expression. He took what he felt was a safe guess at what Ryan was thinking. "He doesn't like having to bring Greta in any more than we do."

"What the hell is this now?" Jack angrily demanded. "Since when did *you* start taking Ryan's side against Greta?"

Daniel swung around to face Jack. Jack was the oldest, but that didn't automatically make him right. Daniel had already butted heads with his half brother over the way he and Greta were training the horses. Now it seemed he would have to fight yet another battle against his father's namesake.

It just went to reinforce the fact that he had always felt like the outsider when it came to the family. Though he resembled his half brothers in his general features, the fact that he was one-quarter Cherokee sometimes made him feel isolated.

"All I'm saying is cut him a little slack. Ryan did everything he could to prove me innocent when everything pointed to me being a suspect in that assault a couple of months ago. And I'm not against Greta. I'm just not against Ryan for doing what he's supposed to be doing as a police detective."

"And what's that?" Jack asked. "Breaking up the family?"

"No," Daniel maintained stubbornly, "finding who's behind all these break-ins and this murder. Now, if you really want to help Greta, why don't you try helping *him*?" Daniel suggested.

"You bucking to be a lawyer now?" Eric asked.

"I'm bucking for the truth," Daniel countered. "Now, if you're not going to help Ryan, at least don't get in his way. Otherwise, we're never going to get to the bottom of all this."

Jack still didn't look as if he had been a hundred percent convinced. "It better be the right bottom," he warned.

Ryan fervently hoped he was going to be able to do that as he left the house.

His first order of business—since he was here—was to have a word with his father to see if the man had changed his story.

There was a time when his father had a mind like a steel trap, Ryan recalled as he went to see him. These days, however, that trap showed signs of being old and somewhat rusted. Still, Big John was lucid more often than he wasn't and Ryan would work with whatever he had and hope for the best.

Finding his father in the study at the main house, Ryan lost no time in putting his questions to the man who had once given every indication that he would live forever. But he had been a lot younger then, Ryan recalled ruefully.

For his part, Big John looked pleased with having the opportunity to talk.

After he took a seat on the soft leather upholstered sofa that faced his father, Ryan got right to it. "Think back, Dad. When was the last time you saw Greta?" Ryan watched his father's face for any signs of vagueness or a wandering mind.

But his father appeared sharp and on point as he answered, "I remember seeing her at her engagement party. She was like a bright, shiny penny, laughing, having a good time. That Mark's one lucky son of a gun, having my girl fall in love with him."

Ryan decided to move the story along a little. Though it pained him to do so, he got to the ugly part. "And then Mom was found…"

Ryan deliberately let his voice trail off, waiting for his father to continue the narrative.

Big John's face darkened from the fateful memory of that awful moment when Jack had called him into the bedroom and he'd seen his wife lying on the floor, bruised and bleeding.

"Some bastard beat her. He hurt my Abra. She was like a broken little sparrow." Tears filled the big man's eyes. He wiped them away with the back of his hand, like a child might. "I find the person who did that, I'm going to break him right in two."

Ryan had no doubt that older or not, his father was still very capable of doing just that.

"No, you'll let the law handle it, Dad," Ryan told him firmly. "The last thing I want is for you to be in trouble with the law, too."

Big J looked at him sharply. "What do you mean 'too'? Who else is in trouble with the law? Is it one of your brothers?" his father demanded. "You know that they can be a little hotheaded at times, but they're all good boys—just like you, Ryan," Big J emphasized. "They've just got a little too much steam to let off sometimes. But boys will be boys, you know that."

"No, Dad, it's not about my brothers." This was really taking a toll on him, Ryan thought. "Now focus, Dad, focus. Was the engagement party the last time you remember seeing Greta here?"

Instead of answering the question, Big J's eyes narrowed, his bushy eyebrows hovering over the bridge of his nose like two furry caterpillars in conference, both vying for the same space.

"What's with all these questions about Greta? Why do you keep asking about where Greta was?" And then, abruptly, it seemed to dawn on him. This time, the two furry caterpillars drew together in obvious anger. "Boy, I don't think I like where you're headed with this. Your sister's got nothing to do with nothing, you hear me?" he demanded, his voice rising.

For a moment, nothing but the sound of Big J's heavy breathing filled the room. And when he spoke again, none of his anger abated.

"I moved heaven and earth to get that girl and I'm not going to stand around, twiddling my thumbs and whistling Dixie while you accuse your sister of doing God knows what. Greta's a good girl, you hear me, boy?" he shouted. "If she says she wasn't in Tulsa, then she wasn't in Tulsa. Don't go turning over rocks, looking for rattlesnakes that ain't there." An edge entered Big John's voice as his complexion took on a definite red hue. "And you leave your sister be, if you know what's good for you."

I only wish I could, Dad.

Out loud, he murmured a cryptic "Good talk, Dad," and walked out of the main house, far more troubled now than he had been when he had first walked onto the property yesterday.

Big J watched his son walk away, forcing himself to put their conversation out of his mind. He couldn't allow it to clutter up what little space he had there. He had to focus on what was ultimately the most important thing in his life.

His wife.

He'd never been a dumb man. Dumb men didn't build up the kind of empire that he had managed to assemble. He knew what was happening, knew that he was slowly beginning to lose bits and pieces of himself. He'd beaten back opponents time and again, but this was one opponent that he wasn't going to be able to win against. In the end, time had a way of bringing all of them to their knees, making beggars out of kings, broken old men out of former proud, undefeated warriors. In his case, it was not his health but his mind that was being stolen from him. He hung on and fought as hard and as long as he could and he intended to go on fighting until the day came when he finally forgot what it was that he was fighting for. Because he wasn't fighting just for himself, he was doing it for Abra.

After all, he was her protector, especially now, when she was so very fragile. He couldn't be her protector if he just gave up and faded into some shadowy world where memories existed in fragmented pieces with entire sections missing.

He didn't want to go there. He wanted to be here, with his lovely princess. It was his fault her spirit had been as delicate as it was. When he'd married her, it wasn't because she'd captured his heart or because he was even a little in love with her. It was because marrying her had been a good business match. Marrying Abra meant gaining her father's property which in turn meant doubling his own. That was the prize to him back then.

He'd been too young and too stupid to realize that while land was what you left as your legacy, the true prize was the love of a good woman. He'd done nothing to earn her love and slowly, though she never said anything, he knew that Abra must have realized that he didn't love her, not then, anyway.

Still, she'd stood by him, done her wifely duty and given him four sons and a daughter. And he, in turn, had added a love child to that mix. A bastard son by a woman who had temporarily won the passion that should have been Abra's.

That had broken her, he thought, affected her health and made her less than the mother to her children than she should have been. Growing up, she was hardly involved in their lives, hardly knew them. Choosing, instead, to travel and be away from them.

And that had all been his fault.

In a strange twist of fate, as the years went by, he found himself loving her more and more. So much so that when that unspeakable attack on her had happened, he thought he'd go crazy with grief and kept vigil by her hospital bed, waiting for the moment when her eyes would finally open again. He wanted to be the first person she saw.

Concerned, his sons and daughter kept encouraging him to take it easy, to go home and rest. How could he rest at home when his heart was elsewhere?

And now she was conscious and home. And bit by bit, things were coming back to her. She was his Abra again.

He just didn't know how much longer he could continue being her Big J.

But he couldn't think about that today. Today he could still remember her the day she became his bride and so could she. They were joined in that mutual memory, together then, together now.

That was all that mattered.

Ryan gave himself till the count of ten, then counted to ten another two times as he got into his car. That had been a frustrating interview with his father, but he finally got his temper under some sort of control. Only then did he start up his vehicle, pointing it back toward town and the precinct.

It took him a little longer before he felt calm enough—or at least relatively so—to place another call to his sister.

Part of him was angry at her for putting him in this sort of a position—the other part of him desperately wanted her to give him something to work with so that he could prove her innocent of all these misdeeds. He really wanted peace to be restored to the family, but he had a sinking feeling that it just wasn't going to happen.

"Where are you?" he asked the second he heard Greta's voice on the other end of his cell phone. He had his phone temporarily mounted on his dashboard, his hands on the steering wheel as he drove back to the precinct.

"I'm still in Oklahoma City, the same place I was the last time you called. Why?" she asked with a laugh, then teased, "You miss me, big brother?"

He didn't engage in the banter she was tendering. Instead, he went to the heart of the matter.

"Then you don't know?" He really wanted to give his sister the benefit of the doubt, but at this point Ryan just couldn't manage to keep the accusation out of his voice.

"Know what?"

He could hear the confusion in her voice. Or was that just part of the act? "That Kurt Rodgers was found shot to death in the bunkhouse yesterday morning."

Ryan heard his sister stifling a cry of horror. Like her confusion, it sounded genuine, but then Greta had been the star of her high school play. He knew that she could be very convincing when she wanted to be.

And avoiding the death penalty was quite a motivator, he couldn't help thinking.

"Do you know who did it?" she asked him in a voice that wasn't quite steady.

"Not yet. But I'm working on it," he answered in a flat tone, then added, "I want you at the precinct by five o'clock."

"Why?" she asked, clearly bewildered. "You think

I can help you find who did this terrible thing? I don't know anything, Ryan. I left Tulsa right after the engagement party. I only came back when I heard that Mother was in the hospital and I left after she regained consciousness and was released."

Ryan wanted to shout at her, to tell her to stop pretending. He wanted to tell her that so far, she was the only suspect he had. But he didn't. He refrained, keeping everything all safely bottled up inside of him until he thought he'd explode from the pressure of keeping it all within.

"Just get here," he told her sternly. "And come up to my floor."

"I'm a little busy right now, Ryan, but I'll be there as soon as I can," she promised, adding, "I want to help any way I can. Kurt was a sweet man and he had tremendous potential. He was so great with the horses." Ryan thought he heard her hesitate for a moment before hanging up. "Is there anything else?" she asked.

Yes, there's something else. Bring Preston with you. You should have a lawyer present when we go over this because, heaven help me, if you did this, I can't let you get away with it.

The unspoken words burned in his throat, as did other words, other warnings Ryan wanted to shout at her.

But those were words that came to him as her brother. There was no room for that here. In this case, he wasn't her brother, he was a homicide detective, dedicated to the single cause of finding perpetrators and bringing them to justice. That was his job, his purpose. His *only* purpose. Issuing warnings to sisters wasn't part of his job description and would only get in the way of his doing the right thing.

The law-abiding thing.

Which, in the long run, he couldn't help thinking, didn't always turn out to be the *right* thing.

But that wasn't his to differentiate.

Chapter 9

Greta found herself feeling oddly ill at ease, considering the fact that she was waiting for Ryan, not only her brother but someone she had always had the very best relationship with. Granted they fought when they were younger, but that was to be expected in a family the size of theirs. Like all her brothers, Greta knew that she could always turn to Ryan if she had a problem.

But there had been something strange in his voice, a strained note she had never heard before. Maybe the job was getting to him.

Or maybe it was the fact that one of the ranch hands had been killed.

Part of her uneasiness stemmed from the fact that

she *knew* that no matter what name might be whimsically attached to the room she was presently in, she was sitting, her hands folded, her back arrow straight, at the rectangular table of what was, quite plainly, an interrogation room.

Not an interview room, or a conference room, but an *interrogation* room.

And she wasn't a fool. She was sitting here, waiting to be *interrogated* by her brother, the homicide detective, about a murder that had occurred on the ranch.

For the life of her, Greta had no idea why.

Until just a few hours ago, she had been vaguely aware that some really strange things had been going on at her beloved ranch, the ranch where she had spent her childhood. But she hadn't been on the ranch for a good part of the time that these things had been happening. She'd been busy with preparing for her wedding.

Under any circumstances, since she had worked with Kurt, she would have assumed that Ryan would want to question her about the ranch hand—she still couldn't get herself to believe that Kurt was really dead. But why Ryan had insisted that he wanted her here rather than just talking to her over the phone was something that continued to eat away at her. It just didn't make any sense.

And, she had to admit, she found it somewhat disturbing.

For the most part, Greta knew that her big brother wasn't a completely by-the-book police detective, but maybe the powers that be were cracking down at the precinct. Maybe *that* was why she was here, but she wished he had told her as much instead of letting her stew like this. The Ryan she had grown up with would have given her a heads-up about all this.

This made her more aware than ever that, sadly, she and her brothers were no longer really that up on each others' lives, the way they had been when they were all kids.

Fidgeting, Greta glanced at her watch. This was cutting into her time, but she'd gone along with Ryan's request because she felt she owed it to poor Kurt. If the ranch hand had actually been murdered, then she wanted justice for him. He deserved nothing less than that if she had anything to say about it.

Greta focused on that aspect of her being here and not on what, if she allowed it, could really get under her skin and bother her: the fact that Mark hadn't offered to come with her when she'd called him about this. She'd told her fiancé about Kurt's murder and that she was going to Tulsa to talk to Ryan.

To her surprise, the man she was going to be exchanging vows with had opted to let her come here alone—apparently never once thinking that she might need a little emotional support. Or at least not saying anything to that effect—or even asking about that possibility.

Greta frowned to herself. She was beginning to have some grave doubts about her pending nuptials and she didn't know if it was just a pronounced case of cold feet or if her gut instinct was trying to warn her of something far more serious.

Tyler, Mark's older brother, the man she had initially come to work for in Oklahoma City, training his horses, was beginning to strike her as a far more compassionate, caring person than Mark was. This despite the fact that if the two were compared, Tyler, who was the president of Stanton Oil, was far busier, with a great many more responsibilities to occupy his time and his mind than Mark. Even so, *Tyler* had time to offer her a shoulder to lean on when she needed it.

Shifting impatiently, wishing Ryan was here already so they could get on with this, Greta unconsciously chewed on her lower lip as she thought back to the other night when she had done a little more than just lean on Tyler's shoulder. She'd opened up too much and said some things that she'd immediately taken back. But she had a feeling it was too late. Tyler had seen the unhappiness in her eyes. She knew he had by the way he had looked at her just before he left.

It made her wonder if she was making a mistake in marrying Mark. What she found herself feeling for his brother was…complicated.

Really complicated, Greta thought with a really deep sigh.

She had a lot of soul-searching ahead of her before the wedding, Greta told herself. Shirking that chore would be nothing short of dishonest, not to mention that she just might be sentencing herself to a lifetime of frustration and an eternity of feeling really unfulfilled.

Greta pressed her lips together in the silent, sealed-off room.

Maybe she needed to postpone the ceremony until she worked all this out in her own mind. But the very thought of postponing the wedding and all the repercussions that action would have sent a very cold shiver up and down her spine.

Her poor mother, who was still recovering from that nasty beating, would have absolute *heart failure* if she even suspected that the wedding might be called off or put on temporary hold.

This was the closest she and her mother had been in a while—possibly ever—and part of her felt that her mother was looking forward to the wedding more than even *she* was. To suddenly pull the rug out from under the woman by announcing that the wedding was being postponed would just be too cruel to do, Greta thought.

Damned if she did and damned if she didn't.

Maybe it *was* just cold feet.

Or maybe—

The door opened just then and Greta's head jerked up, turning toward the sound. She saw Ryan come walking into the room.

A very grave-looking Ryan.

Had he actually aged prematurely for some reason in the past month, or was it just the somber expression on his face that was making him look older?

"Ryan, what's wrong?" Greta asked. Her mother had been attacked and her father was clearly deteriorating. If there was something going on with Ryan as well, she didn't know if she could stand it.

Ryan dropped a file folder onto the shiny, dark gray tabletop. "You mean other than Kurt Rodgers being murdered?"

"Well, yes, of course." The words spilled awkwardly out of her mouth. She couldn't recall ever seeing her brother looking this austere, this unyielding. "What I mean is—you look as if there's something *personally* wrong."

Sitting down, Ryan pulled his chair up closer and looked at her for a long, drawn-out moment. "Maybe there is."

Was there something else going on that she wasn't aware of? She felt her stomach muscles tightening. "Ryan, you're making me feel nervous."

The expression on his face gave none of his thoughts away. "Are you, Greta? Are you nervous? Why?"

This was *not* the Ryan she had grown up with.

"Ryan, you're really beginning to scare me. Please, what's going on?"

His eyes never left hers. If anyone had asked him at the beginning of the year, he would have sworn that he knew his sister inside and out, knew what she was thinking before she did. Now, he wasn't so sure.

"I was wondering that myself. Wondering that a *lot*," he told her with emphasis.

She was starting to think that this job with the police department was not only stressing her brother out, it was changing him into someone she didn't recognize. She didn't want to feel this way about Ryan.

"Maybe we should do this some other time." Greta rose to her feet, gathering up her purse. "I've really got things—"

"Sit down, Greta," Ryan ordered, his voice low, gravelly. But the authority in it was ringing out, loud and clear.

Greta sank back down, doing as she was told. Waiting.

With precise movements, Ryan opened up the folder and began spreading out the eight-by-ten color photographs that were contained inside in front of his sister. They were crime scene photos that the CSI unit had taken, documenting not just Kurt's murder but the break-in at the stable and a couple of the other crime scenes that had occurred on the ranch before that.

When he had finished putting them side by side in

front of Greta, he asked pointedly, "Do any of these photos look familiar to you?"

She looked from one photo to the next. Some of them were painful to view, like those of Kurt's body and the inexcusable vandalism and graffiti that had marked the stables and some of the walls.

She took a breath and raised her eyes to his. "Those are all photographs taken at the ranch," she finally answered.

Ryan inclined his head. That wasn't what he was going for. "What else?"

Greta reviewed the photographs for a second time, feeling ever sicker, right down to the pit of her stomach. When she raised her eyes this time, she saw that Ryan was watching her carefully. Why?

"Just what do you want me to say?" Greta finally demanded, becoming angry.

"You can say whatever you want to say," Ryan told her. He continued studying her, hating the thoughts that were going through his head. Hating the fact that he was in this position and that she had put him there.

"Okay, you want more of a description? Fine," she told him impatiently. She pushed forward two of the photographs, turning them upside down and moving them in front of Ryan. "That's poor Kurt and that looks like the stable that Daniel told me was broken into. Anything else?" she asked.

Ryan leaned back slightly in his chair, crossing his arms before his chest. "You tell me."

She suppressed an exasperated, nervous sigh. "Ryan, I don't have time for a game of cat and mouse."

"Neither do I, Greta," he told her, then decided that maybe it was time to get down to business. "Why did you do it?"

Her brow furrowed. What was he talking about? "Do what?"

And then her eyes widened, opening so far that for a second, it looked as if her very eyes might fall out. "Are you actually accusing me of killing Kurt? Really?" she demanded, verging on speechlessness.

"Did you?" Ryan asked her, never raising his voice above a whisper.

Horrified, Greta had to hold herself in check to keep from leaping to her feet. "No!" she cried.

"Okay," Ryan replied. "Convince me." It was an obvious challenge. "Where were you between the hours of 10:00 p.m. and 2:00 a.m. two days ago?"

It took effort to keep her complexion from reddening. "I was home."

"Tulsa home, or Oklahoma City home?" Ryan asked.

She didn't have to pause to think. She knew exactly where she had been. "Oklahoma City," she ground out. "Can I go now?"

He didn't answer her question. Instead, he continued asking her his questions. Continued closing in on her. On his sister. He felt absolutely sick about it, but he kept pushing because he had no choice.

"Was anyone there with you?" he asked.

She hesitated for a moment. Ordinarily, she could just cite Mark as her corroborating witness. But Mark hadn't been there that night. She had her suspicions about where her fiancé had actually been, but she didn't have any hard-and-fast proof—it had never occurred to her to get that, just as it had never occurred to her that she might need an alibi for any reason.

"No," she finally said, answering the question even though it was really hard for her to say this. "Mark was out of town."

Ryan had seen the hesitation in her eyes. It made him wonder if she was protecting Mark for some reason. "You're sure about that?"

This time she answered Ryan with unwavering conviction. "Yes, Detective Colton, I'm sure. *Now* can I go?"

He felt as if *he* was the one who had been pushed into the corner. But, it didn't matter what he felt about it. He had a responsibility to face up to.

"I'm afraid not, Greta. I've got to hold you overnight for further questioning."

She stared at Ryan, waiting for him to tell her this was all a joke. But no such confession was forthcoming. She felt something cold grip her heart.

"You're serious?" Greta cried, her voice almost breaking.

"Yeah," he told her none too happily. "I'm afraid I am."

Greta felt as if she was totally shell-shocked. It was as if the ground had just opened up beneath her feet, sending her plummeting. "Ryan, how can you possibly think it was me?" she demanded, incredibly hurt.

He tried to remain detached, even though the big brother in him wanted desperately just to protect her, to tell her that it was going to be all right.

"Well, for one thing, your prints were found in the vicinity of the dead man."

"It was the bunkhouse," she pointed out, remembering what Daniel had told her when he'd called to fill her in on the details. "*Everyone's* prints were in the vicinity," she protested.

But Ryan wasn't budging. "Right now, you're our prime person of interest. Now, if someone could vouch for your whereabouts—" It was almost a plea this time, and Ryan watched her face, hoping for a glimmer of a breakthrough.

Greta opened her mouth, as if she was going to say something, but then she closed it again.

She couldn't go that route. It would open up a Pandora's box she *knew* she wouldn't be able to close again. And besides, she really wasn't at liberty to open that box in the first place. There would be a severe penalty to pay, not to mention that Tyler Stanton had only been with her for a few hours, not the entire time in question.

Greta looked down at her folded hands. Ryan could have sworn she looked as if she was praying. "No," she finally said, "I was alone."

Ryan sighed. This was killing him. He wanted to tell her she was free and to go home, but he had rules to follow. "Have it your way. Greta Colton, I'm placing you under arrest for the murder of Kurt Rodgers. You have the right…"

His voice droned on as he said the familiar words to the one person he never thought he would be saying them to.

Ryan stopped abruptly when he thought he heard a quick rap against the one-way glass that ran the length of the interrogation room.

Greta looked at him, as if hoping for some sort of an eleventh-hour reprieve.

He did his best not to look his sister's way as he went toward the door. "Take her to the holding cell," he told the uniformed policeman standing to the side.

"Not to booking?" the man asked.

"No, not yet. We can hold off on that for today," Ryan said, still avoiding making eye contact with his sister. Maybe he was hoping for a miracle after all.

The police officer stood behind the woman he'd taken charge of. "You want me to cuff her, Detective?"

"I don't think that'll be necessary," he told the officer. "She won't try to escape."

With that, he turned a corner, going to the area that was behind the one-way glass.

He wasn't completely surprised to see that Susie was standing there. She had obviously watched the entire session. He knew she would.

"That you playing at being Woody Woodpecker?" he asked, referring to the tapping sound that had brought him out here.

Susie didn't bother returning his cryptic banter. This was far too serious for her to engage in wordplay. Instead, she asked, "You're arresting Greta?"

Ryan scowled, immediately on the defensive. "Don't give me a hard time, Howard. You were the one who said she found DNA evidence placing Greta at the scene of the crimes."

A wave of guilt passed over Susie. She couldn't deny her part in this, but she could defend it. "Yes, but I thought you'd hold off doing anything until we found an explanation for it being there."

He looked at her intently, knowing the answer to the question he asked her even before he asked it. "Well, did you?"

Susie looked really crestfallen to have to admit this. "No."

He tried not to look at the hopeless side of the issue. "Well, neither did I."

Susie sighed as she watched through the glass as

the police officer Ryan had charged with her care took Greta from the room. "Where's Mark?" she asked. "I was sure I'd see him here."

Ryan spread his hands helplessly. "You got me. Greta said he wasn't around the night in question, so it goes without saying that he can't be her alibi."

"I heard that part," Susie said, dismissing it. "But I'm asking why isn't he here now, getting her a lawyer, putting up her bail? What kind of a fiancé *is* he?" she asked.

"Don't get me started on that, Susie," Ryan growled at the very thought of the man his sister was engaged to. "The man is a worthless pile of—"

Ryan caught himself before he became too descriptive. He was supposed to be impartial here.

But the problem was, as Greta's brother, he was none too thrilled with her choice of a husband. Mark Stanton struck him as a ne'er-do-well who was only interested in money but definitely *not* interested in earning it if that required any actual labor on his part.

Thinking over Susie's question again, Ryan had to shake his head. "But you're right. It doesn't seem right to me, a man not being there for the woman he supposedly loves."

Hearing the comment, Susie slanted a glance in his direction. "There's lot of that going around," she murmured under her breath.

Ryan caught that, but he wasn't sure he'd heard her correctly. "What?"

"Nothing," Susie answered quickly. "Listen, I'm going to get back to the lab. There's got to be something we've overlooked that'll point us in the right direction—and hopefully prove your sister innocent."

"Right now, I'm afraid you're a lot more optimistic than I am," he admitted.

The corners of Susie's mouth curved ever so slightly as she paused in the doorway and looked at him. "You're just finding that out now?" Susie asked him. "I never thought of you as a slow learner, Ryan Colton. Guess I was wrong."

She left him in the corridor, trying to puzzle her last words out.

Chapter 10

"Talk about putting in long hours. I didn't think you'd still be here."

Ryan's comment was addressed to the back of Susie's head as he paused in the doorway to peer into the lab. He'd been on his way out when he'd doubled back to see if there had been any new findings.

Susie looked up from the high-powered microscope and glanced over her shoulder toward the doorway.

"I could say the same thing about you," she said to Ryan.

Turning back to the microscope, Susie paused for a second to rotate her head from side to side a couple of times. Her neck muscles felt as if they were starting to cramp up. The tension there went straight up to the top of her head and then spread out. It was beginning to interfere with her being able to work.

"It's *my* sister who's in a holding cell as a prime murder suspect," Ryan pointed out, as if that explained it all.

"And it's my findings that made her a prime suspect." Which was why she was still here, searching for something to disprove her previous conclusions. Taking a momentary break, Susie looked at him again. "Any new evidence?" she asked, assuming that was what had brought Ryan to her lab at this hour.

"No," he replied, successfully keeping the mounting frustration out of his voice. "Any new findings with the old evidence?"

This was beginning to feel like a table tennis match, she thought. Or possibly a stale comedy routine. Susie sighed.

"No." Pushing aside her own wave of frustration that was growing within her, Susie had a possible suggestion for the detective before her. "Maybe you should have another go at Greta."

Bad idea, Ryan thought, her suggestion creating an instant, protective reaction from him.

"And what?" he questioned, wondering just what the woman could be thinking. "Try beating a confession out of her?"

Susie's temper flared, but she clamped it down,

cutting Ryan some slack. It had to be rough, having to accuse someone he cared about of murder. "No, I meant have another go at her about her alibi."

Ryan looked at the forensic expert, clearly confused. "I thought you were listening in earlier when I questioned Greta. She has none."

"I *was* listening in," she told him. "That's why I made the suggestion. I think Greta might have an alibi."

Well, that made no sense to him and his expression said as much. "Okay, if she has one, why the hell wouldn't she tell me about it?"

Sometimes Susie wondered how men had wound up being the ones in charge of things. They only thought in a straight line and they couldn't see what was just beneath the first layer.

"Because she's uncomfortable about it, that's why. I was watching her face when you asked her if anyone was with her that night. Instead of answering you right away, she hesitated."

Ryan shrugged his shoulders, not seeing why that was so important. After all, this was Greta, not some crafty, subversive con artist. "Maybe she was just trying to remember if Mark was or wasn't there on the night in question. Or maybe she was just embarrassed to admit that he wasn't there. They could have had an argument and she didn't want to talk about it. There are a hundred reasons she could have hesitated like that."

But Susie wasn't convinced and she shook her head. "Uh-uh, it wasn't that kind of a hesitation."

Why was she playing this game? It was a game, wasn't it? Jerking him around until he wasn't sure what day it was. Maybe he deserved it, Ryan reasoned, but not during a murder investigation and certainly not during one that, at least currently, involved his sister.

"I didn't know 'hesitations' came in kinds," Ryan fired back, unable to keep the note of sarcasm out of his voice.

"*Everything* comes in kinds," Susie countered.

That still didn't make any sense to him, but Ryan decided to give the woman the benefit of the doubt—after all, she was the head of the crime lab and he did have a healthy respect for her skills.

"Okay," Ryan slowly conceded, "then maybe Greta was weighing her options and decided that if she used Mark as her alibi and the prize-winning jerk really hadn't been there that night, she knew he wouldn't lie to save her from a possible prison sentence. He'd look out for his own neck. And that would make her out to be a murderer *and* a liar." The skeptical look in Susie's eyes was still there, which told him she wasn't buying his explanation. "Okay, so what's your big theory?" he asked.

It was really very simple, Susie thought. "I think she's not giving you a name because she's protecting someone."

Ryan's brow furrowed. "Who?" he asked, curious. "The killer?"

She hadn't worked out all the details yet. "Possibly," Susie allowed. "But I think it's more a case of her being with someone she knew she shouldn't have been with."

"'Been with?'" Ryan questioned, still somewhat puzzled. Was Susie saying what he *thought* she was saying? His frown deepened. "Do you mean like in the biblical sense?"

That was one way to put it, Susie thought, amused despite the gravity of the situation that they were discussing.

"Maybe," Susie allowed. "Maybe not. Maybe even in an innocent sense. But the hour had been late, maybe even actually closer to morning than to night, and that isn't exactly something a respectable young woman does when she's engaged to be married to someone else. She doesn't spend time, alone, with a man who isn't her fiancé. Not if she's still intending to marry her fiancé."

Every time he thought about the bastard Greta was marrying, a wave of close-to-uncontrollable anger would wash over him. Greta had been here a number of hours. Nobody had heard a word out of Stanton. It was probably exactly what Ryan thought—Stanton was just interested in covering his own back. That meant that if Greta went down for this murder, Mark didn't want to be caught in the undertow.

"Who still hasn't come to the precinct to find out why she's been picked up for questioning," Ryan all but growled as he pointed out that glaring fact.

She would have to be deaf not to have heard the animosity in his voice. "I take it you don't like the man."

Ryan laughed drily. "And I take it that you have a gift for understatement."

Susie smiled a little at his comment. "Sometimes," she answered, rotating her neck again and moving her head from side to side. It didn't help.

The tension in those muscles just refused to abate. She might as well give up. The next moment, Susie almost jumped when she felt Ryan's hands on either side of her neck.

"Take it easy," he told her, holding her in place rather than dropping his hands and stepping back. "I'm not about to strangle you. I just thought I could help you."

"I don't understand," she said, trying to turn her head to look at him. But his hands remained where they were and they held her in place. "Help me with what?" she asked.

"I can knead some of that tension out of your shoulders," Ryan answered. "Seeing as putting in long hours on my sister's case is what probably made you so tense in the first place, I figure I owe you something for your hard work."

She was about to protest his interpretation of how

she came by the tension that was causing this severe ache in her neck, but the next moment, Susie swallowed her words. There was no point in denying what was obviously true. And even if feeling his hands on her instantly brought back memories of a happier time—memories she *really* didn't want to have resurrected—she was adult enough to keep those thoughts at bay.

Because if she did allow herself to go there, to remember all that, angry recriminations would find their way to her lips and she would wind up asking him *why* he had done what he had.

Why had he just decided, out of the blue, that he could live very well without her when she had barely survived without him? Had it all been *that* one-sided? Had she really been that much of a fool, to have loved him with all her heart and soul while he had only stayed with her as long as he had because she had been something different, a new conquest for him to acquire and then just move on from?

She refused to submerge herself in those thoughts, because they had been, and always would be, her own personal, private hell. She had no time for hell. Her work schedule was much too full.

Susie tried to shrug his hands off, but he held her in place.

She heard him whistle softly to himself. "Damn, I've felt softer bricks than what I'm feeling while I try to work your shoulders. Maybe you should see someone professional about that," he suggested. She expected him to laugh then, but he didn't.

"Maybe I just need to solve the case," she countered defensively. "And you need to find more evidence—or go at Greta again and find out if she is hiding something." She rephrased it so that it no longer sounded like a foregone conclusion.

This time, she managed to successfully shrug Ryan's hands off. There was just so much resistance and self-control that one person had before they just succumbed—and that would have been a big mistake.

There was a note of irritation in Ryan's voice when he retorted, "I already told you, I didn't get the impression that Greta was hiding anything."

Turning around from the counter, she faced Ryan squarely. With some of the latest technology on her counter whirling and creating background noise, she gave her former lover a long, penetrating look, as if she was trying to read his thoughts.

"Then maybe you need to look closer," Susie suggested quietly.

His patience, always in short supply, began to evaporate at this point. "The world isn't one great big complicated conspiracy, Howard. Sometimes what you see is what you get."

"And what you see is a guilty Greta?" Susie marveled, surprised. If anything she would have thought things would be the other way around—that she

would be the skeptical one he was trying to convince of his sister's innocence. Instead, she was trying to convince *him*.

He didn't want to believe that Greta was guilty,
but at this point in the investigation, he really didn't
know if his sister was guilty or not. He didn't have
anything but his gut to tell him that she wasn't.

And, he thought, *let's face it, I'm not the Pope.*
Which meant he wasn't infallible. Sometimes, he
added sadly, he was all too fallible.

"I hope to God not," he finally said to Susie in
response to her question just before he walked out
of the lab.

But instead of leaving the precinct and going
home, Ryan made his way through the building to
where his sister was being held.

Though his expression didn't change, or indicate
what he was feeling, it really did break his heart to
see her like that.

Ryan couldn't help thinking that she looked like
a lost waif. Despite her height—five-nine—behind
bars his sister looked like a lost, frail waif to him.

He was relieved that the uniformed policeman
he'd sent with Greta had listened to his subsequent
instructions and had put his sister in a holding cell
away from any of the other jailed women who were
spending the night behind bars, courtesy of the
county.

Ryan waited until he had crossed to Greta's cell

and was standing right at the bars before he asked his sister, "Did you make your one phone call?"

Greta brightened instantly when she heard her brother's voice. Looking up, she quickly rose from the cot she had been sitting on and made her way over to the bars to get as close to him as she could, under the circumstances.

She shook her head, her dark brown hair moving back and forth across her shoulders like the fringes of a curtain as she did so.

"No," she answered honestly.

Ryan stared at her, stunned.

"No?" he echoed. Was she kidding? *Everyone* used their one phone call. "Why not?" he demanded. "Why didn't you call someone?"

Slim shoulders rose and fell in a helpless, heart-wrenching movement as she shrugged in response to the question. "I couldn't think of anyone to call," she said. It was a lie, but she was too embarrassed to tell Ryan the truth, that Mark hadn't responded to the message she'd left for him. She needed to re-think things, to deal with them once she was out of here. But that wasn't Ryan's problem, it was hers.

God, but he felt like an ogre. After all, *he* had been the one to put her in here.

"You could have called Dad, or Jack." Ryan pointed out her logical choices. "Or you could have at least called Preston, our family lawyer, so he could have posted bail for you."

But Greta shook her head again, vetoing her brother's suggestions. "I didn't want Dad or Jack getting upset—and Preston would have called Dad to let him know what was going on. Dad's still shaken up by what happened to Mother, and finding Kurt dead must have been an added blow to him—and to Daniel," she threw in, since Daniel had worked closely with Kurt just like she had. "I didn't want to add to everything they were already dealing with."

That was thoughtful, but it really wasn't like Greta, Ryan couldn't help thinking. The Greta he had grown up with and knew was feisty. She wouldn't have taken anything lying down and she *never* surrendered, even if it meant getting their lawyer to do the fighting for her.

This woman on the other side of the bars sounded docile and, worse, defeated.

And you're not helping by accusing her of murder, a voice in his head jeered. He struggled to block it out. It wasn't easy.

"Did they bring you something to eat?" Ryan heard himself asking.

The question sounded lame to his own ear, but he wanted to make sure that Greta was eating. In her present state of mind, he wasn't sure of anything when it came to Greta.

She shrugged indifferently. "I'm really not hungry, Ryan."

He wasn't going to let her just waste away. "You have to eat, Greta."

"Maybe later," she told him, "when all this is behind me."

He thought of what Susie had said and tried another approach. "Greta, are you *sure* nobody can vouch for you for that night? Nobody saw you, talked to you, came over for a while?" *C'mon, kid, give me something to work with here.*

"No," she said with emphasis.

He saw a glimmer of a spark in Greta's eyes and thought that maybe Susie had it right. Maybe Greta *was* covering for someone.

"I already told you," Greta insisted. "I spent the night alone. Why do you make it sound as if that's so unusual?" she asked. And then she turned the tables on him by asking, "Did *you* spend the night alone two nights ago?"

He didn't answer her question. What he said was, "I didn't kill Rodgers."

Her chin shot up in a defensive movement, something the old Greta would have done. "Neither did I."

Ryan tried again. He had to break through the wall she had erected around herself. "If you're lying to protect someone, that's all well and good when it's just a matter of destroying your reputation, or not rocking the boat. That's your choice. But it's not just a matter of that, it's bigger. A hell of a lot bigger. This is the *death* penalty we're talking about, kid," he stressed. "You've got to think of yourself, Greta. The first person you owe something to is *you*," he insisted. "And then it's to Mother and Dad. Think of what this is going to do to them, to lose you all because you have some twisted sense of loyalty."

Greta pressed her lips together and for just a glimmer of a second, he thought he had gotten through to her.

But then he heard her say, "I was alone," and his heart sank.

"Have it your way," he said, his voice distant.

With that, he turned on his heel and walked away.

The prison door, separating the cells from the outer corridor, slammed behind him, emphasizing the separation.

Maybe a night in the holding cell would do her good, he thought. Maybe, if she spent the night there, listening to the echoing sounds of catcalls and whatever else transpired there at night, it would scare her into speaking up for herself.

Because he had a feeling, after this second go-round with Greta, that Susie was right about her hunch. He had come away with the same impression: Greta was holding something back.

Whether it was the identity of someone who could serve as her alibi or something else, he didn't know. But the one thing he felt he did know was that Greta was not being completely honest. His sister was holding something back. And if it was something that could ultimately clear her of all this, then he intended to find out just what that "something" was.

He had to make her tell him.

He hadn't meant for it to happen.

He had always prided himself on the fact that no matter what he was feeling, he always had everything under control. Everything was contained to such an extent that no one ever guessed what he was really experiencing inside.

All he had to do was keep walking, blocking his own thoughts until such time as he could deal with them and they were no longer of any consequence.

Once she was married to his brother, then Greta would be, in essence, his sister, which in turn made her doubly off-limits.

Just place one foot in front of the other, walking in a path directed away from her, that was all that he had to do. Place one foot in front of the other and he'd be home free.

But he didn't *want* to put one foot in front of the other, at least not on a path that led away from Greta. Quite the contrary. In fact, the simple exercise had very nearly taken him in the completely opposite direction.

It had almost taken him to her.

More specifically, it had taken him to her house. After some soul-searching, he'd decided to come to alert her to the fact that maybe marrying Mark was not in her best interest, nor was it the smartest thing for her to do at this time in her life. He wanted to tell her that it wasn't just that Mark was small-minded, petty and even jealous of the woman he was going to marry—it was that Mark was openly cheating on her, as well. His younger brother was making no effort to hide it and certainly no effort to stop it.

Greta deserved better and he had really wanted to turn up on her doorstep to tell her so.

But as he got within five feet of her doorstep, he had second thoughts. If he warned her, if he told her not to marry Mark, then she might think he was just saying that because he'd fallen in love with her himself. And maybe she'd be right, he thought ruefully. Pretty funny, considering that he had never even entertained the notion of having another half to add to his own. But though he tried to tell himself it wasn't the case, somehow, when he wasn't looking, Greta had managed to become his other half.

A half he was having trouble envisioning giving up.

Chapter 11

She knew it was him.

The second that Susie heard the knock on her front door, she knew it was Ryan.

It wasn't anything unusual about the way he knocked, no unique way of rapping his knuckles against the wood to some inner rhythmic beat that had once been a code known only to the two of them. They hadn't been together long enough at the time to develop something like that.

She just knew.

It was as if something inside of her had been waiting for him. Waiting for this moment.

And now it was here.

Dressed in just the jersey and a pair of cutoff

shorts she slept in, Susie quickly made her way to the front door and swung it open.

"Hi." Still holding the door, she stepped back, opening it wider.

The cop in him reacted automatically and he frowned. She hadn't asked who it was and from the sounds he could make out on the other side of the door just before she had unlocked it, Susie hadn't bothered looking through the peephole, either.

"Kind of careless of you, don't you think?" Ryan asked, coming in. "Just opening the door like that without bothering to see who it was first?"

Her careless shrug had the neckline of the jersey sliding off to one side, exposing a bare shoulder as it hung on her, askew. "I had a feeling it was you."

The simple statement caught him off guard. "Why?" he asked. "Am I that predictable?"

He used to be. For that small island of time that they had been together, his reactions had been very predictable. But he had lost his predictability, not to mention any ability to actually feel something other than anger, since then.

"No, I just had a feeling." Since he had come in, she closed the door and flipped the lock into place, mainly out of habit. "Besides, Conway didn't growl." She nodded toward the black-and-white border collie on the floor, who was lying so flat he almost blended in with the rug. "You might recall, he's generally not too keen on strangers coming up to my door."

Conway had been a puppy back then, one she had rescued from an animal shelter less than a month before they first met.

"I recall he was a lot more energetic back then." Squatting down next to him, Ryan petted the dog. "How old is he now?"

There was affection in her eyes when Susie looked down at her pet. "Conway's almost twelve—and he likes to save his energy for things that count."

"Don't we all, boy?" Ryan said, nodding as he ran his hand along the animal's muzzle.

The dog perked up a little, then licked Ryan's fingers by way of a greeting before putting his head down again. His tail thumped a few more times against the floor. And then, just like that, the dog was fast asleep again.

Ryan observed the process with fascination. "He really drops off, doesn't he?" he asked the woman who had just knelt down across from him. Amusement curved his mouth.

"Gotta get those naps in when he can," Susie responded.

She reached over to pet her beloved confidant and companion. She had poured out her heart to the dog—and only the dog—when she'd received the letter from Ryan that had broken that heart into a million pieces. And she could have sworn at the time that Conway seemed to sense what she was going through. In the days following her receipt of the letter, Conway hardly left her side. He seemed to know that she was suffering because of the breakup. Because she had no way of calling Ryan to find out why he had written what he had.

Conway had been there when she first learned of the consequences that arose from falling in love with Ryan—and the price she was forced to pay.

Her mother had been privy to that part of it, to the consequences and what came afterward, but at the time that couldn't be helped. Although she dearly loved her mother, some things she would have rather kept to herself. That had been one of them.

Because they were both petting the dog at the same time—a slightly smaller than medium-size dog—it was one of those inevitable things one of them should have foreseen happening sooner or later.

It happened sooner.

Susie's fingers brushed up against his. She pulled her hand back as if she'd touched fire, then chided herself for reacting like a pubescent teenager instead of a mature adult woman with a master's degree in criminology and an entire criminal investigative department to command.

"He's saving up his strength for the more important things," Susie added matter-of-factly, doing her best to cover up her momentary lapse.

She was fairly certain that Ryan had seen her involuntary shiver the second they had inadvertently made contact.

Rising, she deliberately ignored the hand Ryan offered to help her to her feet. For a split second, she avoided eye contact. She was actually looking at the wall above his head as she said, "Since you're here, it saves me the trouble of having to call you."

Ryan's focus returned to Greta and the case and he was instantly alert. "Something new come up?" he asked hopefully.

"Not quite," Susie confessed. She didn't want Ryan getting his hopes up. "Let's just say something new on something old."

What the hell was that supposed to mean? It sounded like some kind of a riddle. "Let's say something a little clearer than that," he suggested tersely.

Susie started again. "After you left the lab, I took another look at the crime scene photos. Specifically, at the victim's face."

He didn't see how that could have helped. "Okay. And…?" Ryan let his voice trail off, waiting for her to fill in the missing words and shed a little light on where she was going with this.

"And the expression on his face was shock," Susie told him. "Pure, unadulterated shock." And what she was going to say to him next was based on that.

"Getting shot in the gut'll do that to a man," Ryan commented wryly.

Ryan wasn't getting it, she thought. Susie gave it another try. "I'm talking about shock like he suddenly realized that something was wrong."

"Something *was* wrong," he said impatiently. "Greta shot him. I still don't see how his expression is some sort of a revelation," he told Susie, waiting for the new twist part.

Realizing that she wasn't making herself clear, Susie gave it one more try. "No, not as in shock that the woman he'd been working so closely with would suddenly turn on him and shoot him, shock as in the person who was shooting him wasn't the person that he thought she was."

Ryan shook his head, as if the simple action could help clear it and make sense of what she was saying. It didn't. "And the difference is…?"

Patiently, Susie explained it to him. "The difference is that the person who shot him *looked* like Greta but wasn't Greta." There was no flash of enlightenment across Ryan's face so she kept on explaining the theory she was developing to attempt to explain what might have transpired. "Your sister's a very pretty woman, but she's not one-of-a-kind-unique pretty. It wouldn't be hard to resemble Greta enough to be able to pass as her—if someone wasn't paying strict attention."

Much as he wished he could just go along with what Susie was saying, the way he saw it, her explanation left out one very crucial—and damning—piece of the puzzle.

"And the DNA?" Ryan pressed. "The DNA *you* verified over and over again? How does that turn out to be the same as Greta's if the person who shot Rodgers and did all those random acts of vandalism *wasn't* Greta?"

"I'm still working on that," Susie admitted, seemingly not as daunted as Ryan thought she might be, given the circumstances. "You'll be the first to know when I come up with something. You want anything to drink?" she offered, moving away from the sleeping dog on the floor in front of them.

What he caught himself wanting was a tall, cool drink of her, but he knew better than to say that and he was grateful that his internal censor had kept the words from reaching his lips. He'd completely lost the right to do anything other than repent when it came to matters involving Susie that were even remotely personal.

"No, I'd better not," he finally told Susie. "I just might not stop at one," he added honestly. "But you go ahead if you want."

She laughed softly, shaking her head at his instruction. "Haven't you heard? Drinking alone is a sure sign of a problem drinker." Not to mention that if she drank, she might let her guard down and say all the things to him that she had kept bottled up within her for a very long time.

"Okay, back to Greta," she declared with feeling in order to keep herself from veering off track and saying or doing something she was bound to regret. "I know what the evidence says, but none of this makes any sense," she insisted. "*Why* would Greta suddenly do all these insane things?"

She faced Ryan squarely now, treating him like a witness rather than a police detective. "Did anything traumatic happen recently to set her off?" she asked him. "You'd know that better than I would. Did your father suddenly decide to cut her off or did your mother get into an argument with her, saying she was making a huge mistake marrying Mark Stanton?"

"No and no," Ryan replied, answering each of the two questions separately.

Susie had more. "All right, did Greta suddenly have some kind of a meltdown?"

Again Ryan shook his head and said, "No."

There was another possible explanation for Greta's sudden unbalanced behavior. "Has she ever been diagnosed with a mental illness?"

"Not that I know of. Greta's the most levelheaded person that I know."

"Then I stand by what I said," Susie reiterated. "Greta's suddenly turning on a man she worked with and actually shooting him just doesn't make any sense. She's not an irrational person."

"Maybe Rodgers caught her by surprise and came on to her," he suggested. "When she rebuffed him, he just came on stronger and wouldn't take no for an answer."

She could see that scenario—all except for the ending that Ryan was heading for. "A simple slap, or even a well-placed jab with her knee comes to mind. Why grab a handgun and shoot him?" she asked. "Greta struck me as someone with a healthy respect for life."

"You think someone's framing her?" Even as he asked the question, he wanted an alternative to Greta being guilty so badly that he seriously began to entertain the idea, even though logically it made no sense at all.

"It'd be tricky, but it could be done. Does your sister have any enemies?" she asked.

Ryan shook his head. "Not that I know of, but I'm not really all that close to her anymore," he had to admit. Ryan regarded the situation for a long moment, mentally mapping out his next move. "Maybe I'll put that question to her so-called loving fiancé."

"The same man who hasn't been to see her once in the five days she's been in jail, at least not as of an hour ago?" Susie asked, unable to keep the contempt out of her voice.

To satisfy her own curiosity, she had asked to see the precinct's sign-in ledger. No one had been by to see Greta except for Ryan during the entire length of her incarceration.

In Susie's fierce opinion, a leech like Mark Stanton should be kicked to the curb instantly.

Much as it pained him to come out on the side of a man he found himself loathing, in all fairness Ryan had to point out, "I don't think he even knows she's in the holding cell. Greta refuses to call anyone and tell them where she is."

"Being stubborn isn't a bad trait," Susie pointed out in Greta's defense—and possibly her own, as well. "Sometimes, that's the only way things get done around here."

"I never said it was a bad thing," Ryan told her. For just a moment, their eyes met and held and he felt things stirring within him. Things that shouldn't be stirred, not for either one of them.

Ryan abruptly rose to his feet. "Maybe I'd better go."

She knew she should just nod and let him go. That would have been the smart thing to do. Heaven knew it would be for the best because every second Ryan was here like this just seemed to wear down her resistance a little more, even though he probably had no idea what he was doing to her. But she just couldn't keep letting things go. Somewhere along the way, she had to take a stand, draw a line in the sand.

Or yell out the single word. "Why?"

Realizing how shouting that had to sound like an accusation—which, in truth, it was—Susie quickly changed the import of her words by adding, "Did I say something wrong?"

"No, you didn't say anything wrong," he assured her. And then, because she continued looking at him for an explanation for his abrupt departure, he fumbled and told her the truth, something he had meant to keep to himself. Something that, once said, gave him away. "It's—it's your perfume."

Susie looked at him in confusion. "Perfume? I'm not wearing any perfume."

"Cologne, then," he corrected in helpless frustration. "Whatever it is, it's the same one you used to wear, and for some reason, it just seems stronger tonight."

More seductive tonight, he added silently. The truth of it was, the scent he detected was clearly getting to him. It was undermining his senses—making him, in effect, crazy.

Crazy about her.

Or at least more than he already was.

"I'm not wearing cologne, either," Susie informed him.

She made sure she kept busy all the time. Things like remembering to spray on cologne somehow just fell through the cracks. It had never actually made her priorities list to begin with.

"It might be the soap I use," she suggested, unable to think of any other possibility. "It's the same one I've been using ever since I was a kid," she added, thinking that was probably what he was referring to. Nothing else suggested itself to her. "Maybe that's it."

"Maybe," he agreed. Ryan moved toward the door, more for her sake than his own. Susie followed him, remaining much too close to him for his comfort. "Look, I'd better go before…"

"Before?" she repeated. When he made no effort to add any words of explanation to the sentence that was dangling between them, she asked, "Before what?"

Why wasn't he opening the door? Crossing the threshold? Making his getaway? Why did he keep on standing here, as if his feet were glued to the rug?

"Before I do something I shouldn't."

It was a full-out warning to her.

Her brain fairly screamed, *Run!* But her feet remained where they were, firmly planted on her floor. Her heart began to beat a little faster as her eyes met his. Her own voice sounded almost surreal to her as she asked, "And that is…?"

His eyes never left hers. "Do I really have to spell it out?"

It was, she knew, a rhetorical question. Even so, she had to answer, "Yes."

The look in her eyes broke through the last flimsy wall he had surrounding his swiftly weakening self-control.

"Oh, damn it, woman, you should have just let me walk out the door," he told Susie, surrendering to the huge crying need he felt growing within him like some sort of unbridled storm—a storm gaining in breadth and momentum with each moment that went by.

The next second, the yearning within his soul had engulfed him and exploded.

Ryan was as much its prisoner as he was hers.

After pulling Susie to him, his mouth came down on hers and he kissed her the way he had fantasized about kissing her for the past four years, from the first moment their paths had crossed again.

For longer than that.

Very possibly from the moment he had forced himself to write that letter to her, ending, he now fully realized, the best damn thing that had ever happened to him.

Her.

Somewhere in his head, he had attempted to convince himself that his past actions had all been for the best. Just as he tried to fool himself now by saying that all he wanted was to kiss her just one more time and then he could walk away.

But it was a lie and he knew it.

Because kissing her one more time was the reason that he discovered he *couldn't* walk away. Kissing her once made him want to kiss her again.

And again.

And again.

Each kiss was hotter, more ardent, more demanding than the one that had come before it.

Each kiss lasted longer, pulled him in closer, made him want her that much more.

Things became blurred. For now, he felt no shame in the fact that he was aware of kissing her as if his very life depended on it, aware of her softness yielding to him, melding against the hardening contours of his body.

He became aware of his blood heating and rushing through his veins. Became aware that his last ounce of resistance had been shredded into tiny, microscopic pieces. Became acutely aware of the fact that the entire universe began and ended right here, with this woman, inside this kiss.

He heard her breath becoming louder, bordering on being almost erratic.

The very sound excited him almost beyond limits. He hadn't thought that was possible, but then, he hadn't thought that he would ever be able to kiss her again, either.

Drawing his mouth away from hers, he wanted to give Susie a chance to say "no." To push him away the way she should. To put him in his place, which would have been tantamount to hell if he had to be there without her. But she had the right to do that and he deserved anything she wanted to do to him.

He really wanted to give her that chance, to actually *be* noble for once in his life instead of just pretending to himself.

But the second he drew his lips away from hers, the volume of his hunger almost immediately consumed him and he began to kiss every other part of her. Her neck, her cheeks, her eyes. Every available part of her, and more and more of her was available to him as she melted into his being.

Ryan pushed her jersey up over her head, tossing it aside like an inconsequential rag. His eyes feasted on what he had uncovered.

She was, he decided without any reservations, magnificent. His hands felt almost clumsy as they slipped over her breasts, taking possession.

Her sigh of surrender undid him entirely.

Chapter 12

The dog made a noise, as if protesting the fact that he was an unwilling, albeit temporary spectator who had been roused from his sleep by the movements and noises coming from his owner.

The border collie's furry eyebrows rose, first one, then the other. And then, the next moment, Conway's eyebrows had returned to their dormant state, as had he. The dog had gone back into the arms of sleep, content to be there, away from the madness of strange humans.

Susie saw Conway's momentary movement out of the corner of her eye and was grateful that the dog had gone back to sleep. She was afraid that the slightest interruption would cause Ryan to rethink his actions and stop what he was doing—and she didn't want him to stop. She felt as if she was on fire and needed for this to burn through to its natural conclusion.

Having been ignited—admittedly it had taken very little to get her to this heightened, extremely sensitive state—she matched Ryan movement for movement, caress for caress.

Passionate kiss for passionate kiss.

She was well aware that they were swiftly stoking one another's fires and that, very quickly, they would be bringing those fires to their exceedingly logical conclusions.

She wanted this to go on forever. At the same time, her body felt as if it was begging for that final explosion, that final moment where absolutely everything was right with the world and nothing would interfere with that.

Nothing would ever be wrong again.

She'd been dressed skimpily to begin with and Ryan had separated her from her shorts and jersey in less than a heartbeat. Getting him out of his clothes had taken longer, but she was more than a little inspired and there had been absolutely no resistance forthcoming from either his belt or the zipper on his jeans.

Or him.

She couldn't even remember when or how his boots had come off. All she was really aware of, beyond the hunger swiftly gnawing away at her, was that they were both naked, dressed only in their own desires and mingled traces of sweat.

And then, without any further impedance, the hunger burst out in full force on both sides.

Somehow, again without any sort of clear recollection, they had managed to wind up in her bedroom.

That had probably been Ryan's doing, she'd thought later. It was so like him to attempt to give her a small measure of privacy—away from the front window and the dog—and to provide her with some simple comforts. The bed was wide and a great deal more comfortable than the living room floor or even the sofa.

They took turns as to who did what to whom.

It had rapidly turned into a game of one-upmanship. Except that, though nothing was actually said, no audible words actually exchanged, they both knew that it wasn't a game.

But even so there was most obviously an unspoken goal and that was being the one who could give the most amount of pleasure.

That was one of the things she had loved about Ryan. He was a kind, selfless lover, putting her needs above his own. Making her feel cherished and beautiful without saying so much as a single word out loud. It was in the way he looked at her, in the way he touched her. In the way he made love to each and every part of her.

It was the memory of this that she had tried so hard to bury.

And this was what she remembered.

Whenever she had thought of Ryan, she tried to cling to the memory of the pain she had felt when she had read his letter and realized he had abandoned her. Abandoned her just when she needed him most.

But though the pain had been strong, it didn't serve as a barrier, because it dissolved whenever she remembered what they'd had. The glorious way he could make her feel in just an instant. Just because he was there.

As she gave herself up to this wondrous sensation, she knew that no matter where she went, no matter who she met and who she thought she loved, this much would remain constant: that Ryan would always be the love of her life.

The only man she could ever love.

He lost himself in her. He couldn't help it. He wasn't and had never been the kind of man who lived for his next conquest, for the next challenge that crossed his path. Sex had never been a priority for him—except with her. If this had been anyone else but her, anyone else but Susie, he could have stopped it before it had come to this.

Hell, he wouldn't have ever *started* this.

But there was something about this woman that reduced him to a mass of worshipful needs. There always had been, right from the very beginning.

As urgent as these needs were, Ryan managed to

hold himself in check enough to go slower than his body demanded. He wanted Susie to know that this was special—that *she* was special. And making love with her in this even tempo was the only way he had of showing her.

But with all his good intentions, there were human limits and he had come to his.

Kissing her lips over and over again, he gathered Susie beneath him. With his heart pounding madly—in rhythm with hers—he raised his head just enough to look at her face, a face that, years ago, had become the center of all his dreams.

He saw her eyes flutter open, as if she could actually *feel* his eyes on her. The moment she looked at him, his eyes held hers.

And then he made them one.

Time froze.

And then, slowly to begin with, they began to move in concert, each mimicking the other as anticipation gave way to sensation and a surge pushed through them both that was beyond description.

Sharing the moment, heartbeats intertwined, arms tightening around each other, they let the euphoria sweep them away.

Slowly, ever so slowly, the warm mists receded, slipping off into the darkness.

He didn't want to leave, not her, not this magical place they had created together. Even so, he knew he should. There were so many things demanding his attention, demanding his time. Not the least of which was the dilemma his sister was in.

But that all required his getting out of bed. Leaving Susie. And he didn't want to. Because once he did, once he allowed the world to come in, the moment, *this* moment, would be gone. And he was afraid of losing it, of losing her.

So he lay there, one arm tucked loosely around her, holding Susie to him, absorbing her warmth, breathing in her essence.

"There is a scent, you know," he whispered softly against her hair when she stirred against him. "I don't know if it's your shampoo, your soap—or just you—but there definitely is a scent about you. Honeysuckle and roses," he identified, taking a guess. "Or maybe magnolias," he corrected, then laughed at his own indecisiveness. "Flowers really aren't my strong suit," he admitted to her.

He felt Susie's mouth curving into a smile against his chest. Sunshine spread out along his skin just beneath her lips.

"That's okay," she told him, her warm breath against his chest causing the muscles in his stomach to tighten almost into a knot. "You have a great many other talents."

Raising herself up on her elbow, she looked at Ryan, knowing that she couldn't make too much of what had just happened. It would be like trying to capture an elusive hummingbird by closing her hand over it. That would crush its essence.

Still, she leaned her chin against the hand that was splayed across his chest, her eyes on his, and quietly asked, "What kept you?"

He had no idea why that sounded so sexy to him. Or why just the sight of her smile had another strong surge of desire pulsing through him.

Ryan didn't bother trying to analyze it, or attempting to unravel the mystery of what there was between them that seemed so strong.

He just gave himself up to it.

Cupping the back of her head, Ryan brought his mouth down to hers and caught himself all but devouring her lips.

The rest was all too predictable, and too delicious, to attempt to dissect. He'd much rather just lose himself in the wonder that was Susie.

Ryan suppressed a groan as he reluctantly opened his eyes. Annoying rays of daylight were attempting to pry their way into Susie's bedroom.

Daylight.

And Conway.

The border collie had obviously decided to check whether his mistress's visitor was still here. When Ryan did open his eyes, he found the dog had his head on the comforter, his snout just barely a few inches away from his own face. The dog appeared to be taking measure of him.

Ryan ran his hand over the top of the dog's head. Conway accepted the tribute.

"I don't remember your dog being a voyeur ten years ago," Ryan said by way of a greeting when he realized that Susie was already awake and watching him.

"He's settled into a routine—my routine, actually—and he's not used to anyone being in my bed but me," she said, trying to explain why Conway was staring at him so intently.

"Good to know," Ryan murmured. His mouth curved just a touch. "He's pretty protective of you."

"He's my security system," she answered, leaning over to give the border collie an affectionate pat on the head. "Right now, I think he's hungry," she guessed.

When Susie had reached over to the dog, the sheet that she had tucked against her had slipped, treating him to a view of her nude upper torso. Ryan found it utterly impossible to look away, despite any fleeting noble intentions on his part.

"So am I," Ryan murmured.

Susie caught his meaning instantly and suppressed a laugh.

"I'm talking about being hungry for food," she pointed out.

"Oh," Ryan acknowledged, showing just the proper

note of embarrassment—although in reality he was experiencing something entirely different.

Susie knew exactly what he was thinking.

"You want to use the shower first, or should I?" she asked in an attempt to start her day.

His eyes slid over her body, a look of unabashed lust all but radiating from him. "I was hoping, in the name of conservation, we could take one together."

"Conservation?" she repeated as if the word needed to be closely examined. "Correct me if I'm wrong, but there's no water shortage in this state."

He pulled her over against him. "Pretend," he whispered seductively against her ear.

It was a while before she was finally dressed and able to get into the kitchen to make him breakfast.

Humming softly to herself, padding about barefoot in the kitchen, she had just taken out her castiron skillet and opened the refrigerator in a search for ingredients when the doorbell rang.

Susie glanced at her watch. "Who would be on my doorstep at seven thirty in the morning?" she murmured audibly under her breath.

"Only one way to find out," Ryan informed her cheerfully.

"Wise guy," she accused as she wiped her hands on the first towel she picked up.

Walking into the living room, where her evening

had in essence begun last night, Susie headed toward the front door.

Realizing that she wasn't going to even bother looking through the peephole—for a CSI, Susie was almost blissfully naive at times—Ryan was right beside her. If there *was* someone unsavory on her front step, he wanted to be there to protect her. He had his doubts about how effective Conway could actually be beyond growling and baring his teeth. Unless, of course, the dog pushed the so-called unsavory type onto the ground and then subsequently fell asleep on him, Ryan thought, amusement curving his mouth.

Her hand on the doorknob, Susie looked toward him, bemused by his close proximity. "Playing bodyguard now?" she teased.

Ryan made no effort to dispel the image. "Why not? Yours is a body that's really worth guarding."

Her smile went all the way up to her eyes before it widened on her generous mouth. "Why, Detective, is that a compliment?"

He laughed, pressing a kiss to the top of her head. "Absolutely."

She'd been teasing, but his answer did warm her heart. For good reason. "That's the first time you ever gave me one, you know."

He was about to contest that, but then, reflecting, Ryan realized that she was right.

"I was an idiot back then," he told her with feeling. And he meant it. It would have cost him nothing to tell her what was in his heart. How she made him feel. He had allowed too many opportunities to slip by. He wouldn't anymore.

Susie laughed softly as her eyes all but delved into him. "You'll get no argument from me," she assured Ryan solemnly.

He knew she was referring to his having sent her that breakup letter—and at this point, he had to agree with her.

The doorbell rang again, more insistently this time. Whoever was on the other side of the door was now leaning on the button.

The jarring sound went all through Susie and she shivered.

She saw suspicion enter Ryan's eyes. He was staring straight ahead at the door. And then he motioned for her to unlock it, his right hand holding his service weapon drawn and ready.

"Just who do you think is ringing the doorbell?" Susie asked in a whisper, amused. Ryan looked as if he was ready to take down a member of some organized-crime syndicate.

"You can never be too careful," he responded in the same hushed whisper. "Open it," Ryan ordered in no uncertain terms, the expression on his face as dark as she had ever seen it.

Taking a deep breath, Susie flipped open the two locks on her front door. Then, bracing herself, she pulled open the door.

She heard Ryan cocking his weapon at the exact same moment.

The person on her doorstep sucked in their breath at the same time that she did.

And then, seeing who it was, Susie's mouth dropped open.

"Mother!" she exclaimed.

Chapter 13

She had a master's degree in criminology, was a thirty-year-old top forensic expert who headed her own CSI team within the Tulsa PD and had managed, through diligent, tireless work, to crack a number of exceedingly difficult cases. Yet, even so, in less than two seconds in her mother's presence, Susie felt as if she was an awkward ten-year-old child in mismatched shoes.

Her mouth was completely dry as she cried, "Mom, what are you doing here?"

Short and petite, Elizabeth Howard's ordinarily bright, sunny face darkened instantly as she gazed right past her daughter's head and straight at the dark-haired young man standing just behind Susie.

"Apparently, having a heart attack. What's *he* doing here?" Elizabeth demanded, then immediately held up her hand, as if warding off her daughter's answer. "No, never mind. Don't say it. I don't want to hear it." Her brown eyes narrowed, boring holes into the object of her fierce anger. "I can figure it out for myself."

"Mrs. Howard," Ryan began, having absolutely no idea what he was going to say to follow up on his opening salutation.

He never got the opportunity even to shakily make an attempt.

Elizabeth, far more diminutive than her daughter, went after him like a piranha that had been on a forced starvation diet for the past month.

"You have one hell of a nerve, showing your face here after what you've done, Ryan Colton—"

"Mother!" Susie cried, raising her voice in a desperate attempt to drown her mother out until she could find a way to get the woman to subdue her temper.

"No, it's okay," he told Susie. Turning toward her mother, he said, "Mrs. Howard, you have every right to be angry at me."

Elizabeth's brown eyes had narrowed into almost fiery slits. "I don't need your *permission* to think of you as the scum of the earth, a heartless bastard who doesn't even have the decency—"

"That's enough, Mother," Susie warned, an angry edge entering her voice.

There were equal amounts of anger and pity in her eyes, both wrapped in a mother's love, when Elizabeth looked at her daughter.

"No, it's not enough. It'll never be enough," Elizabeth said hotly. "Are you forgetting that he *left* you? Left you and then wrote a Dear John letter to break up with you instead of facing you and telling you in person like a man?" The daggers returned as she turned her glare back toward Ryan. "But then, a real man wouldn't have run out on a woman when she was pregnant with his baby, now would he?"

"Mother!" Susie cried, utterly appalled that her mother would have just shouted out her secret so blatantly after Elizabeth had promised never to say anything to anyone, not even her own husband. This was supposed to have been just between the two of them.

"Wait, what?" Dumbfounded, Ryan stared at the woman he had just spent the night with. There had to be some sort of a mistake. "You were *pregnant*?" he asked her, stunned.

Elizabeth snorted, not taken in by what she viewed as his act for a moment. "Oh, like you didn't know," she jeered.

"He *didn't* know, Mother," Susie insisted, coming to Ryan's defense.

Just like that, his whole world felt as if it was imploding around him, collapsing in on itself, leaving him to free-float through space like a jettisoned piece of trash. Ryan stared at the woman he thought he knew. "Why didn't you tell me?" he demanded.

He had to ask? Seriously?

Anger became her shield. "I wasn't about to go crawling after you when you clearly didn't want me enough to even write letters to while you were away fighting overseas."

She was bright enough to figure out why he'd had to do it, Ryan thought. "I didn't want you to feel as if your whole life was on hold. I really wanted you to move on."

But none of that, noble or otherwise, mattered anymore.

"A baby," he said, the very word feeling so strange on his tongue. Why hadn't he seen it? Why hadn't she said anything once they had reentered each other's lives? Numb, confused, shocked, Ryan heard himself asking, "What did we have?"

"We didn't," Susie replied stoically, staring straight ahead at the wall above Ryan's head. It was the only way she could even get herself to say the words that were associated with the most awful event that had ever happened to her in her whole life. "I lost her," she finally added, her voice so low that he had to strain in order to hear her.

"Her?" Ryan repeated, feeling shell-shocked and numb at the same time. The words dripped from his lips. "It was a girl?"

"It was a girl," Susie confirmed, her voice only the tiniest bit louder than when she had initially told him about the loss.

Something twisted inside his chest, skewering the organ that was supposed to be his heart. "Oh, God, Susie, I'm so sorry."

Elizabeth's expression indicated that she didn't believe him for a moment. "Yeah, right. Easy to say now that it's all over. I'm sorry, honey," she told Susie. "I don't buy the crocodile tears. He should have been here for you when you needed him."

"You're right. I should have," Ryan said with sincerity to her mother.

There was nothing he could ever say that would make up for what had happened. In all honesty, he had no idea how to ever set things right. Ryan felt as if his very presence was only serving to agitate her.

It was certainly agitating her mother.

"Look, I think that I'd better go," Ryan told her in a subdued voice just before he turned on his heel and walked out the front door.

"Ryan—" Susie began, starting to hurry after him. She was stopped by her mother, who caught her by the arm when she tried to hurry past the woman.

"Let him go, Susie," Elizabeth ordered. "He wasn't here for you when it mattered, and he has no business sniffing around you now."

Susie turned to confront her mother face-to-face. "Mother, I said he didn't know."

Elizabeth frowned. "How convenient. He didn't know because he cut off all communication with you."

Susie sighed. She could see that this argument would go around in the same tired old circles.

Even so, she was bound to defend Ryan, especially after what had just happened last night.

"He had his reasons," she told her mother, in effect defending the very action she had taken apart and scrutinized so many times in her heart herself.

Elizabeth laughed shortly. "Yeah, it's called self-preservation, so that he was free to go tomcatting around anytime he wanted to."

Susie closed her eyes, seeking strength. "Ryan's not like that."

"Honey, they're *all* like that," her mother maintained with authority. "Except your father, of course, but that's probably only because he knows what I'm capable of doing if I ever found out," she said without any particular fanfare.

"Mother," Susie said pointedly, "Ryan lost a child, too."

Elizabeth refused to be swayed or impressed. Most of all, she refused to view anything about the man who had broken her daughter's heart in a favorable light.

Susie could see her mother digging in. Susie had inherited this stubborn streak from her. "They're not all alike," she insisted.

The laugh was a little harsher this time. Elizabeth Howard was not a woman given to illusions. She dealt in reality.

"The one that isn't is on display in the Smithsonian, under glass," Elizabeth informed her sarcastically. She put her fisted hands on her hips, as if that could somehow help her understand her daughter's flawed thinking. "Why would you even let that man inside your house?" she asked.

Susie paused for a second, trying to find a way to phrase her answer acceptably. What she wanted to say was *Because I love him,* but she knew that would only lead to an argument, which would, in turn, really upset her mother.

So instead, she said, "We were going over a case."

Elizabeth looked at her knowingly. "Is that what they're calling it these days? A case?"

"Mother, it wasn't like that," she said, knowing that if she told her mother the real truth, she would never hear the end of it until the day that one of them was dead. "His sister is accused of murder," Susie emphasized.

Elizabeth appeared to perk up for a moment. "Do you think I could hire her to off Colton before she's sent away?"

If she didn't know any better, Susie would have sworn that her mother was serious. "Mother, please stop talking like a grade-B TV procedural and be serious."

Elizabeth looked at her in all sincerity and said, "I *was* being serious."

Susie threw up her hands. It was no use. "What are you doing here, anyway?" she asked, asking the same question she had put to her mother a hundred years ago, when her mother had first shown up at her door. "And please, this time spare me the dramatics."

"I could say the same thing," Elizabeth told her. "I tried to call you last night and you didn't answer your phone."

She must have accidentally turned it off when she and Ryan had started rocking each other's worlds, Susie realized. Retaining a poker face, she told her mother, "I could have been working on a case."

It was a plausible enough excuse. "That's what I told myself. But then I called again this morning and you still didn't answer."

She remembered turning on her phone this morning. The call must have come in while she and Ryan had been in the shower together.

Sparing her mother the longer version, Susie simply said, "I must have been in the shower then."

She saw the skeptical look entering her mother's eyes. "You must have been," the woman agreed without really agreeing.

Despite this little frustrating episode, she really did hate worrying her mother. She could well imagine how she was feeling. "Why were you trying to reach me?" she asked.

"For no other reason than because I couldn't reach you," Elizabeth told her, falling back on cyclical reasoning. Elizabeth frowned now, glancing toward the shut door and obviously thinking of the man who had just gone through it. "Are you going to be all right?" Elizabeth asked, her voice sounding far more compassionate than it had a moment earlier.

Susie shrugged, as if physically attempting to shed the question. "Why wouldn't I be?"

By the expression on Elizabeth's face, a dozen reasons obviously came flooding back to her. Being a mother didn't just stop after eighteen years. It lasted for a lifetime.

"Alphabetically, chronologically or by order of magnitude?" Elizabeth asked.

In response, Susie leaned over and kissed her mother's cheek. "I love you, Mom. There're times I really want to strangle you, but I love you."

"Ditto," Elizabeth replied, her expression giving nothing away. She debated for a moment before speaking again. "Susie," her mother said in a quiet, firm voice, "I want you to stay away from Ryan."

Susie raised her chin stubbornly. She wasn't going to get pulled into an argument with her mother about this, she wasn't. But she wasn't about to let her mother steamroll over her, either. "Can't, Mom. We work together, remember?"

Elizabeth sighed and rolled her eyes. "All right

then, work together," she allowed. "But for heaven sakes, don't play together."

Okay, enough was enough, Susie thought. "Mom, please don't take this the wrong way, but butt out. This is none of your business, really," she told the older woman emphatically.

"I'm sorry, but it is my business," she contradicted. "When the doctor cut the umbilical cord that joined us, she did not cut the part that worried about you, that wanted only the best for you. Sorry, but there's nothing you can do about it. You're stuck with that. And, furthermore, I intend to go on worrying about you and wanting the best for you. The latter, by the way, is definitely not Ryan Colton."

It was getting late, and Susie could practically *feel* the work piling up on her desk even as she stood here. "I've got to go to work," she told her mother, picking up her purse from the table by the front door. "So if there's nothing else—"

Elizabeth held up her index finger. "There's just one thing."

"Yes?" she asked, struggling to suppress her weariness.

"Be careful," Elizabeth warned her, concern etched deep into her features.

"Always," Susie assured her.

"I wish I could believe that," Elizabeth said under her breath. It was still loud enough for Susie to hear. "Call me later," Elizabeth instructed her daughter.

Preoccupied, trying to think of a way to prove Greta innocent, Susie responded to her mother's remark with a murmured "Uh-huh."

Elizabeth would have none of it—and she was not above making threats when it suited her purpose. "Or I'll come over."

She would, too. Her mother had already proven that. "I'll call, I'll call."

"Good girl." Elizabeth paused in the doorway for a moment, looking at her daughter, her only child whom she loved intently with all her heart. "In case I haven't been clear enough, that's an order, Susie," Elizabeth said just before she left.

Susie's sigh was audible even through the closed door after she shut it.

A child.

She'd been pregnant with a child.

His child, and he hadn't even known of its existence until it didn't exist anymore.

The stark reality of that weighed oppressively on him. Ryan hardly remembered getting behind the steering wheel of his car. Barely remembered starting the car and pointing it toward the precinct.

Technically, he had enough time to make a quick pit stop at his house before he went into work. That would give him an opportunity to put on a fresh change of clothes, maybe get something to eat on the fly.

But all those niceties seemed beside the point and of no real interest to him.

A child.

He would have been a father if—

If.

A gut-wrenching, breath-stealing, double-barreled two-letter word that could and did make all the difference in the world to him.

If he had known...

If she had lived...

If.

Ryan blew out a ragged breath. There was no point in torturing himself. He *hadn't* known and now that he did, he couldn't do anything about it to change the circumstances. Couldn't do anything to make it up to Susie, or change the way things had played themselves out.

Last night had shown him that he wasn't over her. Would *never* be over her, and he might as well get used to that glaring fact of life. Some men could move on. Some men actually had more than one love of their life over the course of their existence.

And some men fell just once—and hard—never to experience that wonderful, surging, teeth-rattling feeling again.

He fell into the latter group and it was his misfortune that he hadn't done everything in his power to hold on to Susie, to remain in her life and not allow her to get away, when he had the chance.

Allow?

Hell, he hadn't "allowed," he had pushed, pushed her away with all his might, because he'd thought that was the right thing to do for both her *and* for him. A man worrying about the girl he left back home wasn't razor sharp. He wasn't at the top of his game and it took being at the top in order to attempt survival. Even then, it wasn't a done deal.

So he had chosen to shed everything that might have kept him from making it through the awful experience of war and thus, he had survived.

But survived for what?

To what end?

His life was filled from end to end with work, with making others safe so that they could sleep at night, while he went home to an empty house with an empty feeling in the pit of his stomach.

An emptiness that it seemed nothing, no amount of honor and duty, could fill. Somehow, it didn't seem as if he had managed to accomplish anything at all—other than hurting a woman who might very well have been, if things had gone well, the mother of his child.

The ache Ryan was feeling in the pit of his gut was almost indescribable.

He was here, at the precinct, he abruptly realized as he mechanically pulled into the parking lot.

Ryan couldn't remember how he'd got here.

It was as if the car had somehow known the way, he thought wryly.

Maybe, if he just threw himself into his work until he could face and deal with what he'd just learned, he'd find a way to eventually come around.

Until then, it would be a matter of putting one foot in front of the other, taking one thought and hopefully linking it up to the next.

Provided he could think, of course. As of this moment, the chances of that were rather slim to none. Right now, his entire brain felt as if it was engulfed in some sort of a dense fog. He was unable to see his way clear to anything.

But then—

Ryan stopped abruptly as he realized, getting out of his vehicle, that he was standing only a few feet away from, and staring at, Susie's car.

Somehow, she had managed to have gotten here ahead of him.

How was that even physically possible? He'd driven here straight from her place.

It was enough to make a man feel as if he was irrevocably doomed.

Chapter 14

He should have gone straight to his desk. He knew that.

But knowing and doing just weren't aligning themselves for Ryan lately. Instead of heading for the elevator and pressing the up button, or even just heading for the stairs and going upstairs to the homicide division, the way he did some mornings, when Ryan got to the stairwell, he went down.

Down to the basement. Where the lab was.

Where *she* was.

He still couldn't believe that Susie had somehow managed to get to the precinct ahead of him. After all, he had left her condo first, ahead of her. When he'd driven away, she was still inside, with her mother, presumably still being quizzed by the woman as to what she could have possibly been thinking, spending the night with him.

Granted he hadn't driven hell-bent for leather, more as if the car was on sedatives, but still, he should have arrived here before she had.

Or at the very least, they should have arrived at the same time, their paths crossing in front of the entrance of the building.

Half in disbelief, half drawn as if by some sort of mystical siren song, he went to the crime lab's main door.

The door was unlocked and standing open, as if his presence had been anticipated.

Looking in, he saw her. Susie had just slipped on her white lab coat and was about to slide onto the stool right before her favorite piece of equipment—a state-of-the-art, ultra-high-powered microscope.

He saw her shoulders tense ever so slightly and knew she'd sensed him standing there. Because he didn't want to seem as if he was lurking, Ryan spoke up. "What are you doing here?"

Susie didn't look up. Whatever was on the slide seemed to command her full attention. "I work here, same as you."

Well, he hadn't come to gawk, he'd come to tell her something. Rather than retreat and wait until a later time, Ryan forced himself to speak.

"Listen, under the circumstances, if you'd rather

have your assistant handling this case…" This wasn't coming out right and he tried again. "What I'm saying is that if you have a problem working with me, I get it. I understand."

Very slowly, Susie increased the magnification, just a whisper of a hairbreadth at a time. "I don't have a problem," she told him crisply. "Do you have a problem?"

"No," he answered. He hesitated, trying to find a tactful way to broach the matter he really wanted to talk about.

"Then let's get to work," she replied, her attention apparently still focused on the microscope in front of her.

He couldn't just pretend that he was still in the dark about her former pregnancy and miscarriage, that nothing had been said. When it came to personal matters, under ordinary circumstances, he tried to avoid direct conversations. He would usually just brush things off to the side until they resolved themselves one way or another.

But this was different.

This was far too important for him to pretend that it hadn't happened—or that he didn't know. They had to get this out into the light of day once and for all—and then hopefully clear the air as best as could be expected.

"Look," he began slowly, his tongue feeling like pure lead, "about what your mother said—"

No!

She raised her head away from the microscope and turned around on the stool.

They weren't going to go there. She refused even to entertain the idea of a discussion about the most sensitive topic of her life. Nothing could be gained from going over that painful territory. Certainly nothing would be changed.

"Never mind about my mother," she told him in a tone of voice he had never heard before. "We've got a lot of work to do if we're going to save your sister." Susie glanced at him when he didn't immediately respond or agree. "You remember your sister, don't you? Really cute, with long brown hair and a can-do attitude? Fortunately for her, she doesn't look a thing like you—ring any bells yet?" Susie asked, peering at his face.

Ryan stifled a surge of irrational anger. "Yeah, it does."

"Good." Susie got down to the salient part of the matter. "Because the more I think about it, the more things just don't gel for me. I don't think she's behind any of this. The first thing we need to do is to find a way to get those murder charges against Greta dropped. And we both agree that she's holding something back," she continued, her voice gaining momentum. "I think she was with someone and she's obviously unwilling to tell us who that was.

Would she have confided in one of your brothers?"
she asked, looking at Ryan for some kind of insight.

He shook his head. "They would have immediately come forward if she had—at least they would
have come to me. Everyone in the family dotes on
Greta."

"How about your mother? Would Greta have
confided anything—say, maybe prewedding jitters
or doubts and why she was having them—to your
mother?" Susie felt that the key to Greta's silence had
something to do with her pending wedding.

Again, he shook his head. "Everyone had been
walking on eggshells around my mother ever since
the incident."

That was the way he and the rest of the family
referred to the attack his mother had suffered: the
incident.

Abra Colton had regained consciousness slowly,
and bit by bit, she'd remembered more of the day
of her attack. He was fairly certain that his mother
remembered everything, but he could see that she
didn't want to talk about it. He didn't want to press
her yet, not until he had to. But the truth of it was,
he was beginning to feel as if he was running out
of time.

There were definitely moments when he wasn't
crazy about his job.

"Okay, then maybe one of her bridesmaids or her
maid of honor would know if she was having second

thoughts, or if something was off-kilter for Greta. *Someone* has to know something," she insisted.

Ryan read between the lines. "You think my sister was fooling around with someone other than her fiancé," he guessed bluntly.

It sounded harsh, but these things did happen. "It is a possibility that can't be overlooked."

She knew Ryan would have said the same thing—if this hadn't about his little sister. But then he was the one who had brought Greta in and put her in a holding cell in the first place. Ryan didn't need to have his duty pointed out to him.

Ryan nodded stoically in response to what she had just said. "Okay, I'll go see if I can get any of her bridesmaids to break the code of silence and talk to me about this—if there is a 'this,'" he qualified.

He began to walk toward the exit and was caught off guard when he saw Susie taking off the lab coat she had just slipped on. The next moment, she had crossed over to him.

"What are you doing?"

The look she gave him said that was clearly self-explanatory. "I'm going with you. Why?"

He nodded toward the microscope as well as the other equipment on the granite counter. "I thought you said you had work to do."

"I do, but you were right. Harold can handle some of it." She knew the man was more than eager to flex his lab muscles. "You need backup," she told

Ryan when he continued to regard her quizzically. "More than that, you need emotional support." She allowed a quick, quirky smile to momentarily curve her mouth. "I'd be the one to know all about that."

"Susie—" he began, completely at a loss as to what he could possibly say to her that would make an utterly horrible and painful episode in her life even the tiniest iota better.

"Shut up and walk, Colton," Susie ordered, waving her hand toward the hall and indicating that was where their next steps should take them. When Ryan did just that, moving ahead of her, she addressed his back, adding softly, "You don't have to say anything, you dummy. I understand."

He turned around then, a thousand unsaid things all there in his eyes as he looked at her, possibly searching for forgiveness, if not absolution.

"Susie," he began again, angst, apology and so much more vying for space in his voice.

"You're not walking," she reminded him.

Her tone, although not abrupt, told him she wasn't up for any further discussion of their issue at the moment—maybe never. But right now, it was enough for her to know that he wanted to address it.

Intent carried a great deal of weight with her.

He paused by the elevator. "Maybe I should have another go at Greta before we tackle the bridesmaids."

"Now, *there's* a lovely image," she cracked.

"Maybe if she sees you, she'll be more inclined to talk," Ryan speculated, a note of hope coming into his voice.

Susie gave a noncommittal shrug. "Can't hurt to try."

Retracing their steps back to the elevator rather than leaving the building, they went to the rear of the first floor where the holding cells were kept.

When Ryan requested that his sister be brought to the common area, where inmates were allowed visitors, the uniformed officer, an older man with gray streaks in his hair, appeared to be a little hesitant.

"Something wrong, Sergeant?" Ryan asked. There was nothing unusual about his request. Why was the sergeant acting as if there was glue on the soles of his shoes?

"Not wrong, sir, but the prisoner you requested brought to the common area is already there. She has a visitor, sir."

"You mean someone came by before?" Ryan asked, wanting to get what the officer was saying clear.

"No, now," the sergeant corrected. "She's in the common room talking to—" Pausing for a second, the sergeant looked back at the log to verify his information. "Mr. Stanton."

"Well, what do you know, Mark finally showed up. The lazy SOB certainly took his sweet time about it," Ryan muttered. There was no love lost between Ryan and his brother-in-law to be.

"No, it's not Mark Stanton," the sergeant corrected. "The name on the log is Tyler Stanton."

At the mention of the president of Stanton Oil, Ryan exchanged glances with Susie. Surprise melted into curiosity. Either way, he still needed access to his sister. "I need to see her, Sergeant."

"Very good, Detective," the sergeant obliged. "I'll just tell Mr. Stanton that he has to step aside and wait until—"

"No," Ryan said more forcefully than he intended. It stopped the officer in his tracks. "It might be useful to talk to my sister with Tyler there." Ryan could see that his idea sat very well with Susie.

"Okay, whatever you say, Detective." The sergeant led the way.

Walking into the common area, Ryan took little notice of the other prisoners who were seated at a handful of tables, talking to people from their former daily lives. For the most part, the former group seemed acutely aware that the latter were free to come and go just as they wished.

Ryan's attention was entirely focused on Greta and the man who was seated opposite her. From what he heard as he came closer, Tyler Stanton was taking her to task about something.

The first words Ryan heard were "Why didn't you call and tell me?"

Ryan automatically looked over his shoulder at Susie as a strong feeling of déjà vu washed over him.

"Sound familiar?" he asked her under his breath.

"A lot of people say that in here," she answered crisply, looking straight ahead rather than at him or any of the people at the tables.

"I didn't want to get you involved," Greta stressed in what could have amounted to a very low stage whisper. Her voice was so low that had he and Susie not been almost on top of the duo at the table, Ryan was fairly certain that he wouldn't have heard any of this exchange between his sister and her fiancé's brother.

He heard Susie clearing her throat and had a feeling that she was doing that deliberately, especially when Tyler almost jumped, indicating that he had been completely unaware that there was anyone there, listening to what he was saying to Greta.

When Tyler did realize who was there, his expression took on a whole new demeanor. He looked stunned, and somewhat annoyed, as well. Not at the intrusion, but over what he seemed to regard as an omission.

"You knew better." And then he turned in his chair to face Ryan. "You should have been the one to call me the second she'd been arrested because you thought—" Tyler regrouped, his thoughts scrambling all over one another. "You can't possibly think that she killed that cowboy she was working with," he said to Ryan.

Ryan began the way he always did, citing the facts. "The evidence—"

Usually mild-mannered, for a moment, Tyler lost his temper, his complexion reddening from anger. "To hell with the evidence. She wasn't at the ranch when Rodgers was killed. She was—"

Horrified and clearly surprised, as if anticipating his next words, Greta cried, "Tyler, don't!" Swinging around to appeal to her brother, she begged, "Don't believe him. I don't know why he's doing this, but he's just trying to protect me."

"She's the one trying to protect *me*," Tyler contradicted.

Ryan sighed. This could go on for hours. "Would both of you just stop trying to protect one another and spit it out? What are you trying to say?" Ryan asked, looking from one to the other.

Susie was unable to hold her tongue any longer. "Isn't it obvious?" It was a statement rather than a question because it was certainly obvious to her. Since last night, it felt like all her thoughts were geared toward seeing relationships where none should have existed. After all, she couldn't help thinking, look at her own situation. She certainly shouldn't have allowed last night to happen, yet there was no way she could have humanly prevented it, feeling the way she did about Ryan. "They were with each other." The look she gave Greta was filled with understanding and sympathy. "And it's Mark you're trying to protect, isn't it?" she asked. Before Greta could answer, Susie continued as she warned the woman, "Don't. If you're attracted to Tyler, then you owe it to yourself to call off the wedding until you're absolutely sure about the direction you want your life to go in."

Ryan laughed shortly. "Well, there you go. Out of the mouths of babes," he said philosophically, indicating Susie.

"But it's not true," Greta cried. "He's making it up to keep me out of jail. Tyler wasn't with me," she insisted. "I was alone."

It was obvious that Ryan wasn't buying her protests. Maybe because he wanted to prove that she was innocent, but whatever the reason, he went with Susie's interpretation.

At the moment, his attention was focused exclusively on Tyler. "Now, just give me the short and sweet version—and remember, I want the truth. Were you with Greta during the time in question?"

"Yes," Tyler replied emphatically.

"Tyler—" Greta pleaded.

Ryan held his hand up, silencing his sister. He was still looking solely at the other man at the table. "From when to when?" he asked, wanting Tyler to pin the time down. He did, after all, need facts to back this up.

There was no hesitation in Tyler's voice as he answered the question put to him. "From nine in the evening until seven the following morning. We were—"

Ryan quickly held up his hand again, this time to prevent Tyler from continuing. "I don't need that part," he said, stopping Tyler before the latter could give him any further details. He might be the investigating detective on this case, but he was still Greta's brother and as far as he saw it, there was such a thing as too much information. At least, in this instance. "Short and sweet, remember?" he asked, referring to the format of the details he had requested. "You're willing to swear to what you just said?" he pressed.

"Absolutely," he said without any reservations.

"Tyler," Greta begged, "if nothing else, think of your reputation." She didn't want to be the reason that people walked way from his company or his family turned on him.

Especially since Tyler was lying.

"My reputation is a pretty paltry thing," he told her, "if it means that you have to sacrifice your life for it."

"Well, seeing as how your reputation for telling the truth in these parts is only second to that of George Washington," Ryan went on to assess, "I'd say that gives Greta a pretty damn good alibi." He turned to look at Greta. "But we're still facing that annoying so-called fact that you were supposedly seen in the area around the time in question. That means the eyewitness is either lying—"

"Or they saw someone who looks like Greta," Susie quickly interjected, tactfully omitting the fact that she had already raised the possibility of someone lying about seeing his sister earlier.

Drawing him away from the table, his sister and Tyler, Susie suggested, "Tell you what, why don't we go and question your mother next?" The second the words were out of her mouth, she saw the hesitant expression in his eyes. She knew he was thinking about upsetting his mother and was reluctant to do so. Ordinarily, she would be, too, but this was definitely not something that fell under the heading of "ordinary." "It's the only way we can start clearing Greta's name and get to the bottom of all this. The more information we have, the better our chances are of finding out what actually happened."

It all made sense. Ryan nodded. "You're right," he agreed.

"Of course I'm right. Tell you what. I'll even bring the eggshells."

He looked at her quizzically. "Come again?"

"You said everyone is walking around your mother as though they're treading on eggshells. I get that," she told him sympathetically. "Some people are more fragile than others. I don't want to upset her, I just want to find out why, according to what you've told me, she looks so nervous around Greta every time they're in the same room together when clearly, from all indications, your sister loves her and wouldn't do anything to hurt her for the world."

Ryan wanted to pin down her reasoning so he knew what he was dealing with. "You think it might be this Greta look-alike who's responsible for the attack?"

"Honestly?" Susie asked. When he nodded, she said, "I think we've had enough questions. It's time to look for some answers. And if we have to turn over some rocks and rattle some cages to do it, so be it. The truth is not always easy to get at, but in the long run, it'll be worth it."

Ryan couldn't have agreed more.

Chapter 15

It was her first time at the main house on the Lucky C ranch and Susie had to admit that although she *thought* she was ready, she definitely was *not* prepared for the sight of the 11,000-square-foot brown-and-beige Oklahoma-stone house. Even the outside of the main house was overwhelming.

A circular flagstone driveway lead up to the impressive two-story building. It came with a grand outside staircase that in turn led up to a two-story open foyer.

"Be it ever so humble, there's no place like home," Susie murmured under her breath. She knew the Coltons were wealthy, but this gave wealthy a new meaning, at least for her.

Hearing her comment, Ryan laughed as he haphazardly parked his vehicle at the end of the driveway. "I guess it can be a little overwhelming at first," he agreed.

She slanted a glance in Ryan's direction. "You think?"

At any other time, he might have volunteered to give her a tour of the place, but right now, they both had something more pressing to attend to.

"C'mon, I think I know where my mother is," he told Susie, leading her inside.

"Mr. Ryan, I wasn't expecting you." The surprised greeting came from a silver-haired woman of medium stature. Trim, with gray eyes and her hair pulled back in a severe, tight bun, Edith Turner had been with the family for twenty years, and was in charge of keeping the household running as smoothly as a classic timepiece. It upset the woman greatly that so much turmoil had taken place recently under her watch. Her body posture indicated that she was being even more vigilant than usual.

"I wasn't expecting to be here, Edith," Ryan told the woman by way of a greeting. "Is Mother in the sunroom?" he asked.

Ryan noticed that the housekeeper was scrutinizing Susie, but the woman was much too polite to say anything beyond answering the question she was asked. "Yes, she seems to enjoy spending her mornings there."

Ryan nodded his thanks and made his way to that location.

Susie was right behind him. "She's not very friendly," she observed, glancing back at the woman they left in the foyer.

"She is once she gets to know you," Ryan assured her.

"So I guess she's never going to be very friendly," Susie commented.

Was that just a flippant remark, or was Susie putting him on notice that what had happened last night was a one-time thing, strictly for closure and nothing further?

This wasn't the time, Ryan told himself sternly. He could settle things between the two of them later, once he put this thing with Greta to rest.

"Mother, I brought someone with me," Ryan said as he quietly entered the sunroom.

The woman who had given him life was sitting in a white wicker chair, a delicately crocheted white throw covering her lap and legs to ward off any minor, would-be chill lingering in the air.

At sixty-one, Abra Colton was a remarkably thin, fragile-looking woman who showed no telltale traces of ever having given birth to five children. Thanks to the vigilant efforts of a skilled, faithful, longtime hairdresser, there were no traces of gray evident in her straight, chin-length dark brown hair.

There was an edginess about the graceful woman

that was immediately evident to all but the most casual of observers. It had become even more noticeable in the past few months, ever since she had suffered the attack. An attack she'd suffered in her own home, which had robbed her of any feelings of safety she might have clung to. Now she was never safe, never fully at ease.

Despite that, she did appear to be coming around, albeit very slowly.

Abra shifted her gaze from her son to the young woman who was standing beside him. Sharp eyes took immediate measure of Ryan's companion.

"So I see," Abra replied. "Is she your girlfriend Ryan?" she asked.

Rather than have Ryan deal with what would be an awkward explanation at best, Susie stepped up and handled it for him.

"We work together, Mrs. Colton." Susie extended her hand to the woman. "I'm CSI Howard."

After a beat, Abra took the hand that was offered to her. "CSI?" she repeated, looking from the young woman to her son for an explanation.

"Crime scene investigator," Susie clarified. She couldn't help thinking that Ryan's mother was probably the only person in the country who didn't know what the letters stood for, given the extreme popularity these days of procedural programs.

"Oh," Abra murmured.

Susie could almost see the woman visibly withdrawing from them. What was she afraid of? Had seeing them caused her to remember something? Confront something that had been hidden from her until just now? Somehow, she had to get the woman to trust her, Susie thought.

"We need to ask you a few questions," Ryan told his mother patiently, then added, "About when you were attacked."

Abra stiffened visibly, her entire demeanor becoming defensive. "I don't want to talk about it."

"Please, Mrs. Colton, this is important," Susie stressed. She lightly placed her hand on top of Abra's, making contact. The look in the older woman's eyes told her a great deal. "You saw your attacker, didn't you?" she asked softly.

"No, no, I didn't," Abra cried, growing agitated. "Please, don't ask me," she implored. The plea had been directed toward Ryan.

His natural inclination was to back away, to try to curtail his mother's suffering as quickly as possible. But Susie had been right. If his mother remembered anything at all, *saw* anything at all, she had to tell them.

"Did the person who attacked you look like Greta?" he asked her.

Abra's eyes flew open, as if she was startled by the accuracy of her son's question.

"But it wasn't Greta," she cried. "I know my Greta. This woman's face was contorted with hate.

Greta doesn't hate me," Abra insisted. "She loves me. She said so." As she spoke, Abra clutched at her son's forearm, squeezing it as her agitation increased.

"Take your time, Mother," Ryan urged calmly. "We're not going anywhere."

Appearing sufficiently controlled, Abra took a moment to gather herself together before continuing. "At first, I thought that maybe Greta was on some kind of mood-altering medication, or possibly taking street drugs. Young people do the stupidest things," she confided sorrowfully. "But when she came to see me at the hospital, Greta seemed fine. She was so upbeat, so concerned about me. There wasn't a trace of hostility at all—I was afraid maybe I was losing my mind," she confided. "And then I was just afraid…" Her voice trailed off. When she looked up at Ryan again, it was to implore him for reassurance. "But it wasn't Greta who did this to me, was it?"

Ryan's hand closed over his mother's in a gesture of protectiveness.

"No, Mother, it wasn't Greta."

For a moment Abra looked content, but then her troubled expression returned. "But then who was it? Who was pretending to be my daughter while she was doing such terrible things?" she demanded as forcefully as she was able.

"That's what we're going to find out, Mrs. Colton," Susie promised.

Abra addressed her solemnly, "Please do."

Taking their leave, neither of them said a word to the other until they were in the hall and out of his mother's earshot.

For a moment, Ryan felt stumped. "So what now?" The question was more to himself than to Susie.

"Now we look for someone who's imitating your sister and find out why she's doing it."

Imitating implied an impostor. That still left them with the same glaring problem that had confronted them from the very start.

"And the fingerprints and blood?" he asked. How did she intend to explain the fingerprints and blood that had been found? Or was that an inconvenience that was being swept under the rug for the time being?

Susie shrugged dismissively. "Maybe someone lifted them and then strategically planted the prints where they would do the most harm. Same could have been done with the blood. It's not difficult to envision that."

"Maybe not hard to envision, but tricky and very difficult to execute," Ryan pointed out. "Greta would have to have had some psycho following her around, lifting and transferring fresh prints and smearing her blood when she wasn't looking." It kept coming back to that, back to Greta's fingerprints and blood. There *had* to be another explanation for that being at the crime scene. "There's no other way that the fingerprints and blood evidence could turn out to be identical?" he asked.

"Well, yeah." As far as Susie knew, there was only one other explanation possible for identical fingerprints. "But your sister would have had to have a twin—twins have identical DNA—and I really think you might have been aware of there being twin girls growing up at your house."

Something she said struck a chord for him. Ryan strained for something in the back in his mind. "Maybe not."

Stunned, Susie stared at him. "You're going to have to explain that."

He was still trying to work it out in his head himself. "Something my father said recently that keeps popping back up in my head. At the time we were talking about Greta being a prime suspect in the stable break-in, and he said something to the effect of having gone through a great deal of trouble getting Greta, so he wasn't about to give up on her now. Not *conceiving* Greta, but *getting* her."

Susie didn't see the problem. "Potato, po-tat-toe," she countered. To her "conceiving" and "getting" could be seen as synonymous.

"Hear me out," Ryan said. "Have you ever noticed that Greta doesn't really look like the rest of us?"

"All of you—including Greta—have dark brown hair." The differences he was referring to were only minor. "So her eyes are hazel green instead of bright green." Or, in his case, magnetic green, she couldn't help thinking. "That's not exactly enough to make her stand out in a lineup—or label her a Colton impostor."

He didn't like the word *impostor* but maybe Greta really wasn't a Colton. "But it is possible, right?" he asked.

"Anything is possible," Susie conceded. "I guess the only way to settle this is to talk to your father and find out if he's just being careless with his words, or if that was actually an unintentional slip on his part."

Ryan nodded. He wasn't looking forward to this, but it was something that had to be done. "Let me take the lead on this, okay?" he cautioned.

There was no way she would have fought him for the right to question his father. That task belonged exclusively to him.

"You're the detective," she told him.

"You don't have to come along if you don't have time. This is probably keeping you from your work," he guessed.

She shook her head.

"Uh-uh, I'm not missing this for the world. I'm not leaving until we get some answers about this that make sense."

Ryan felt the same way.

They found Big J in the den.

The silver-white-haired man's back was to the doorway and he was standing in the middle of the room, right in front of his extensive library. He was regarding the books, appearing to be lost in thought.

For a moment, Ryan thought his father hadn't heard them come in and he was hesitant to intrude on the man. But then Big J spoke and Ryan realized that he knew they were there after all.

"You know, there was a time when I knew what was in almost every one of these books. Now I don't even remember why I got half of them."

He turned around to face them, then addressed his son. "Don't get old, boy. It's a bear. Old age is an unkind thief that can rob you of everything that's important to you."

Ordinarily, he'd let his father go on as long as he wanted to. But there was nothing ordinary about his visit to the ranch.

"Dad," Ryan began, interrupting his father, "I need to ask you something."

"Sounds serious," Big J joked. When neither his son nor the woman with him smiled, Big J's own smile faded. "I guess this *is* serious," he surmised. "All right, what's this question you have to get off your chest?" he asked.

Ryan really had no idea how to ask his father this. There was no delicate way to proceed, so after a moment, he just plowed in. "Is Greta my sister?"

Big J stared at him as if he had lost a few screws. "Of course she is. Why? Are you suddenly drawing blanks about things, too?" Big J asked, concerned.

But Ryan wasn't finished. "Is she my sister by blood?" he pressed, determined to get the issue resolved once and for all.

Big J stiffened. Instead of answering, he asked, "Why do you ask?"

"Dad, answer the question first," Ryan insisted. "Is Greta my sister by blood, yes or no?"

Big J hesitated, taking so long to answer that for a moment Ryan thought maybe his father had actually forgotten the question—or perhaps was drawing a blank regarding the answer.

But then—finally—Big J uttered a single, bitter-tasting, judging by his expression—word. "No."

Finally!

"I need details, Dad," Ryan requested gently. His father's answer had him reeling, but this wasn't the time or place to deal with that. This was about a murder on the ranch and proving that Greta wasn't the one who did it.

Big J seemed to deflate right before their eyes, gripping the armrests of his chair and sinking into the soft leather cushion as if his knees could no longer support him.

"I didn't know what to do. That last pregnancy took everything out of your mother. She used up her last ounce of strength giving birth to that precious baby girl and the doctor was afraid that the least little thing might just kill your mother. But the baby wasn't strong. She died the next day."

"Died?" Ryan echoed, stunned.

"The news would have definitely killed your mother. You know what she was like. And she was weakened, besides. I had to do *something*. And then I heard a couple of the nurses talking about this woman who had just given birth to twin girls at home because she was too poor to pay for a hospital stay. I hardly knew what I was doing, but I went to see her.

"The house was like a pigsty," he recalled. "And she was a mess. There was no husband around. I offered to pay her fifty thousand dollars for one of her daughters—and her silence. She gave me her word she'd use the money to move away and promised never to tell her other daughter that she had a twin sister. There was nothing else I could do," he added helplessly. "You see that, don't you?"

Rather than Ryan answering, they heard the crashing sound of a china cup hitting the tiled marble floor behind them.

Whirling around, Susie saw her first. Abra Colton had come up behind them and had listened in silence to her husband's story. Pure shock had caused her to drop the cup filled with tea she'd held in her hand.

"Oh, John, how could you not tell me?" the older woman cried.

Big J jumped to his feet, hurrying to enfold his wife in his arms.

To Susie, it looked as if it was actually the other

way around, that it was Abra who was holding—and comforting—her husband.

"I was so afraid of losing you," the big man cried. "I had already lost my daughter, I just couldn't stand to lose you, too, and you were so weak then, so very frail." Holding her to him, he kissed his wife's forehead. "I'm sorry I didn't tell you, Abra. I wanted to. So many times, I wanted to," he swore. "But somehow, the time just never seemed right." There were tears in his eyes as he pleaded for her forgiveness. "I'm sorry," he repeated.

Abra was visibly comforting her husband.

"There's nothing to be sorry for. You should never be sorry for being kind," she told him gently, hugging her husband again.

Ryan stepped back and let his parents have their moment. Turning toward Susie, he whispered, "Well, on the plus side, this clears Greta of murder *and* those incomprehensible acts of vandalism she was accused of committing."

It was very obvious that Ryan was greatly relieved his sister was cleared. That was what had drawn her to him in the first place, Susie recalled, the way he was so loyal to his family, even though they might not see eye to eye on a lot of things. Her own family was close and that had always meant a great deal to her.

"Yes," she agreed. "I guess all we have is the minor, annoying little detail of tracking down this obviously evil twin before she does any more damage she could pin on Greta. Your sister isn't going to be safe until this other woman is caught."

That hadn't even occurred to him yet. "I guess I've still got my work cut out for me," Ryan said, thinking out loud.

"We," Susie corrected with emphasis. *"We* have our work cut out for us."

Ryan stopped walking. "Are you telling me you intend to come with me and help track her down?"

Susie looked at him as if she couldn't understand how he could possibly think anything else. "Just try to stop me."

Tracking down a suspect wasn't her field. "But you belong in the lab."

"I belong anywhere I want to be," Susie deliberately countered.

Ryan knew when he was on the losing end. He raised his hands in mock surrender. "You'll get no argument from me."

"I guess there's always a first time," Susie said wryly.

They were outside of the main house now and heading back to his car when he pulled Susie to him and kissed her. "I'd rather concentrate on second chances," he told her.

She blinked, trying not to appear shaken. "What was that for?" she asked, referring to the sudden kiss.

Ryan felt that his one-word answer covered it all.

"Everything."

Chapter 16

Greta held her breath as she watched the police officer unlock the door to her cell. She didn't release it until the creaking door was actually standing wide-open.

"That has to be the most beautiful sound I've ever heard," Greta confided to Ryan as he and Susie stood behind the officer who had unlocked the door.

For a moment, Greta stood in the cell, as if afraid to take another step, concerned that it was all a hoax and that the door would be shut on her again before she had a chance to make it across the threshold.

But the guard didn't attempt to close the cell door again. Instead, he continued to wait, watching her impatiently. With what seemed like a burst of energy, Greta quickly strode out of the cell.

"I'm really free," she cried, her eyes all but tearing up with relief and joy.

"Absolutely," Ryan told her. He smiled at her. The relief his sister had to be experiencing was no greater than his own. Just so that she was clear about the dropped charges, he went over the list of things she had been accused of. "You didn't kill Rodgers, you weren't the one to deface that property on the ranch and you didn't attack Mother."

Greta's eyes widened at the very last part of her brother's statement.

"Attack Mother?" she echoed. "Mother thought I was the one who attacked her?" Even as she said the words, it seemed surreal to her.

"Actually no," Susie was quick to interject, slanting a glance at Ryan. Ryan had a great many good qualities, but tact wasn't always one of them. "What your mother said was that it *couldn't* have been you, even though her attacker had your face and looked like a really angry, deranged version of you."

Greta glanced from the forensic expert to her brother, more confused than ever. "Someone looked like me? I don't understand."

"Believe me, I know this isn't going to be easy for you to hear, but—"

Ryan stopped abruptly when he heard the sound of boots coming down the corridor.

About time they got here.

He saw Susie looking at him quizzically, but he didn't want to say anything more until his brothers had reached them.

All four of them were talking over one another, eager to hug Greta and assure her that they were in her corner no matter what.

"Looks like Ryan finally came to his senses and let you out," Brett said, taking his turn at hugging his sister.

"God, but you're a noisy bunch," Susie commented with a grin.

"We would have hired a brass band if we thought we could get it past the sergeant at the front desk," Jack told her, laughing as he gave Greta a bear hug.

"What are you all doing here?" Greta asked. It was clear that she was really glad to see them, especially now that they were all on this side of the cell. "You didn't have to come."

"Yeah, we did," Eric told her. "Besides, Mr. Detective here—" he jerked a thumb at Ryan "—asked us to come here because he had something to tell us. I figure he wants to get the apologies over with all at once instead of telling us one at a time. Am I right?" he asked, his sharp eyes pinning down his older brother.

"Actually," Ryan replied, deliberately stretching the word out for effect, "no. I called you here to tell you the reason Greta's fingerprints were found at the scene of each crime."

It was obvious from the way they all exchanged glances that the brothers had their own opinions about that.

"Because your lab is second-rate and slipped up?" Jack guessed.

Ryan was quick to come to Susie's defense before she had a chance to say anything herself. "Our lab is first-rate and nobody slipped up."

Brett clearly wasn't convinced that Jack's answer was off-base. "Then how do you explain saying that Greta's prints were found at the scene?"

"Because they were," Ryan answered. His eyes darted toward Greta as he told his family, "Greta's got a twin sister."

Daniel stared at his half brother. "Oh, c'mon, is *that* what you're going with?" he cried in disbelief.

Out of all the others, he had been the one who had remained in Ryan's corner, but even he found this excuse to be completely outlandish and extremely difficult to swallow.

"That's what he's going with because it's true," Susie told Ryan's brothers and sister.

It was obvious that Ryan's explanation was still falling short of its mark.

"And what, Greta's 'twin' is invisible, so the rest of us can't see her?" Brett asked sarcastically.

"Oh, you can see her, and you did," Ryan assured

his brother, ignoring the sarcasm. "Mother saw her when she was attacked by her and that other ranch hand saw her arguing with Kurt Rodgers just before Rodgers met his untimely death."

Jack shook his head. "Look, it's nice that you're finally in Greta's corner, Ryan, but even *you* could have come up with a more plausible story than this twin fairy tale."

"It's not a fairy tale, it's the truth," Ryan told them calmly. "You want proof?" he challenged. When his brothers all nodded their heads, the expressions on their faces all daring him to come up with some sort of way to validate what he was saying, Ryan told them, "CSI Howard and I confronted Dad about it and he told us the truth."

"That you're insane?" Jack guessed.

Ryan went on as if he hadn't heard his older brother. "He told us that when Mother gave birth the last time, the baby died the next day. Dad was really worried that the news might send Mother over the edge—she almost died giving birth—so he found someone who had just given birth to a baby girl and offered to buy her. Only problem was, the woman had given birth to *two* baby girls and Dad had to choose which one he was going to pass off as Greta."

Ryan could see that what he was saying had really shaken his brothers—and Greta—up. But he kept pushing on, wanting to get this all out now.

"The woman promised to take the other girl and

disappear. Fast forward twenty-six years, the other twin is no longer 'disappeared,' she's surfaced, and for reasons I can only guess at she's gone on a rampage to discredit Greta and frame her for murder."

"Why?" Eric asked. "Even if we believe this fantastic story you just told us, why go through all this trouble to get Greta discredited?"

Ryan looked at Susie to see if she wanted to take over, but Susie's expression told him that he could continue. She indicated that this was his show.

"Our best guess is that she is angry that Greta got to live the good life while she didn't and she's out for revenge," Ryan answered.

"So you know where this 'other' Greta is?" Daniel questioned.

"Not yet," Ryan told him, adding firmly, "but I intend to find out."

"But if you don't know where this other person is," Jack pointed out, "how can you speculate that you know she's trying to frame Greta to get revenge?"

That part was easy, Ryan thought.

"Think about it," Ryan stressed. "Very few people get to live the way we did and we do. And from what I gathered from just a cursory collection of background information, Greta's and this angry twin's birth mother wasn't exactly up for any Mother of the Year Awards. I'd say that Greta's twin had a rotten upbringing and feels cheated. Why did Greta get to have all the luck," Ryan said, turning to look directly at Greta, "while this twin had to do God knows what to earn a living—not to mention the fact that she probably got battered around a bit by Mommy Dearest."

"But you're just speculating," Eric said, going back to that nagging fact.

"For now," Ryan allowed. "But I've got a hunch that I won't be for long," he promised his brothers as well as Greta. He could see by the look on her face that she was having a hard time absorbing and accepting all of this. "I—we," he corrected, sparing a grateful glance in Susie's direction, "intend to find this woman who's trying to frame Greta and bring her back to face all the charges that had been brought against our sister."

It was clearly a great deal to take in and process. He could see by the expressions on his brothers' faces that some of them were having a more difficult time than others in accepting this far-from-run-of-the-mill explanation.

"And you're sure you're right about this twin thing?" Jack pressed skeptically.

"As sure as all of us are standing here," Ryan said with unwavering certainty to Jack and the others.

Brett shook his head, as if to clear away the cobwebs. "How could Dad have kept this from us for all these years?"

"I'm sure he had his reasons," Greta said softly, coming to the man's defense.

"Yeah," Eric answered. "Mother."

As he said that, it was obvious that a thought had suddenly hit him. It seemed to telegraph itself through the gathering at the same time.

"Does she know? Mother," Brett specified, "does she know, or is she still in the dark?"

"No, she knows," Ryan assured all of them. "She overheard Dad confessing all this to Agent Howard and me, telling us why he did it."

"How is she?" Jack asked, concern in his voice.

"This is hard for all of us to wrap our heads around," Brett interjected. "The news must have just about killed her."

"Actually," Ryan answered with new respect for the woman who had periodically bowed out of their lives for prolonged amounts of time while they were growing up, "our mother is a lot more courageous than we've been giving her credit for. She seemed genuinely touched that Dad had been worried enough about her to do something completely out of his comfort zone just to spare her grief. When I left the two of them, *she* was the one who was comforting *him*."

Greta's mouth dropped open at the image Ryan had just created. "You're kidding."

"No, he's telling you the truth," Susie assured her, stepping in again. "It was all rather sweet, actually. They seemed to be completely committed to one another." A fondness flashed over her face. "You don't always see that with couples who have been married as long as your parents have."

Jack apparently wanted to have the matter—and his fears—laid to rest once and for all. "So this means that all the charges against Greta have really been dropped?"

"Each and every last one of them," Ryan declared with more than a small measure of enthusiasm and satisfaction.

"And exactly what do you intend to do about this evil twin—I can't believe I just said that," Eric muttered, shaking his head. He wanted to be sure that Ryan lived up to his word.

"We're going to find her," Ryan said with unwavering confidence. "At the moment, we can't put an APB out on the woman because people are going to keep trying to drag Greta in, seeing as how Greta and this other woman seem to be sharing the same face, but we'll get her," Ryan promised. He was trying to sound nothing but upbeat for Greta's sake.

Daniel seemed to be trying to share that feeling, but he needed a little help in order to try to sell it. "You seem awfully confident about that."

Ryan tried to remember if his brothers had *always* doubted his abilities as a homicide detective like this, or if this was something new.

Humoring Daniel, Ryan explained, "Now that we know *who* we're looking for and what we're up against, yes, I am. Everyone is bound to slip up once in a while—and I'll be there to catch her the second that this woman does slip up."

"Well, I guess it sounds like you've got your next move planned. Is there anything we can do?" Daniel asked.

"Yeah, try to make this up to Greta for me." He smiled at his sister. She would never know how happy he was to find out that he'd been wrong. "I think I kind of came down hard on you, and I'm sorry. If Tyler hadn't come forward—"

"Whoa, wait a second. Back up here," Jack told his younger brother. "Don't you mean Mark? Mark Stanton's her fiancé, not Tyler," Jack reminded him.

"And he was also a no-show as far as coming up with her bail money, or even just standing by her," Ryan told them, scowling. "Rumor has it he didn't want to be photographed coming down to the precinct. The pig *still* hasn't shown his face around here."

Eric tried to find excuses for Mark. "Maybe jails make him nervous—or maybe you do." Eric took his thought a step further. "Maybe the guy's scared of you."

Brett laughed shortly. "I can relate to that," he said, speaking up. "I'm scared of you."

"In what universe?" Ryan scoffed, waving away his brother's so-called revelation.

Jack's raised voice cut through the cross fire of

conversations. "What's this about Tyler?" he asked. "Just what kind of an 'alibi' for Greta did Tyler Stanton come through with?"

Ryan glanced in Greta's direction. "Oldest one in the world," he answered.

Jack immediately caught his drift and looked at Greta, almost speechless. "Really, Greta? You and Tyler?"

No, not really. But if she said anything to deny the claim, Tyler Stanton—whose only sin was trying to save her—would be disgraced for lying to the public. She knew how very fickle the public could be. They loved their heroes, loved building them up— and loved tearing them down even more.

So for his sake, she fashioned a nonanswer answer. "I'd rather not talk about it," she told her brothers evasively.

She had no idea why, but Tyler had lied for her. More than that, if that fabrication of his was somehow leaked to the press—it would completely unravel her pending wedding.

Would that be so bad? a little voice inside her head asked.

The closer her ceremony came, the less inclined she was to take part in it.

Moreover, the less convinced she was that she actually *did* love this man with the extremely attractive face. On a scale of one to ten, in the looks department Mark Stanton scored a twelve. But in the soul department, such as when it came to all these small details, or recalling the location of their first date—or even answering her phone calls the night she'd been taken into custody—Mark fell painfully short of the goal.

Mark couldn't even put himself out to pay her a visit, while Tyler, for reasons she couldn't begin to understand, had not only put himself out for her, he'd *lied* for her.

Lied to give her an alibi and keep her from being charged with the murder of Kurt Rodgers.

His lying would have quickly come to light and fallen apart if it hadn't been for Ryan. If Ryan hadn't been so committed to proving her innocent, hadn't grasped at straws, Tyler's act of chivalry would have all been for naught and quickly dismantled.

"Does that mean the wedding's off?" Daniel asked his sister as the thought suddenly occurred to him. By the look on his face, he wasn't exactly consumed with worry for his sister.

"I sure as hell hope so," Susie cried, piping up. The others turned to look at her and it was obvious by the expressions on their faces that they had forgotten that she was even there, a silent witness to their conversation. "Any man who doesn't stand by the woman he's supposed to love doesn't deserve to marry her," she said firmly.

"Well, I don't know what the hell Mark Stanton is thinking—or *if* he's thinking," Brett added with a dismissive wave of his hand, "but I can sure tell you one thing for sure, we'll all stand by you," he told Greta, acting as the group's spokesman.

Greta was taking nothing for granted. It had been that kind of a day. "Even after what you just found out?" she asked incredulously.

"That you've got some evil twin running around, pretending to be you?" Eric asked.

"No," she cried. He was missing the point. They all were. "That I'm not your sister."

"The hell you're not," Jack told her. There was no arguing with his tone of voice. "You grew up with us. You fought with us, laughed with us. You were a part of every day. If that's not what makes a sister, well, then I don't know what does. You're a Colton, Greta. You might as well stop fighting it and just come along peaceably."

There were tears in her eyes as she nodded and said, "I guess that's that, then."

"Yes, it is," Ryan told her with finality, adding with a conspiratorial wink, "Remember, Jack doesn't like to have anyone argue with him."

And no one, apparently, was about to argue with Ryan, either.

Chapter 17

Tension radiated from every pore of his body. He'd been at this for hours.

And the end result had been fruitless.

Nada. Nothing. Zero.

Annoyed, Ryan pushed the keyboard away so hard it bounced on his desk before impotently coming to a rest, askew.

So far, all the leads he and Susie had come up with hadn't panned out. They'd either led him around in circles or they brought him smack up against a dead end. Like now.

Dead end.

A little like his own life, he couldn't help thinking. At least, his life the way it had been for the past ten years—and especially as of late.

Hard as he was working to find a lead on this faux Greta—and he was working very hard—Ryan's thoughts kept going back to what he had unexpectedly found out, thanks to Susie's mother and her completely unanticipated visit.

The scene with the feisty, combative woman kept replaying itself in his head.

He'd been a father.

For a small inkling of time, he'd been a father, or rather, a father-to-be—and then he wasn't. And it had all happened without the slightest bit of knowledge on his part. And, to add to the insult and pain, all of this had transpired not recently, but almost ten long years ago.

Ten *years* ago.

The very thought just boggled his mind as he turned it over and over again in his head.

If that baby had had a chance to make it and survive, right about now she would have been about nine years old.

The very idea shook Ryan down to his very roots, not so much that he could have been a father but that he actually *liked* the idea of being a father.

Where had that even *come* from? Ryan silently demanded.

He hadn't felt any stirrings or longings when Jack had had a son. Oh, he really loved his nephew, Seth, and looked forward to doing things with him as the boy grew, but watching Jack and Seth together had never made him particularly enthused about offspring of his own. Or even envious.

Yet abruptly finding out the other day that Susie had been pregnant with his baby, and then lost it, filled every single crevice within him with remorse, with deep, consuming regret and with an unbelievable longing. He certainly wouldn't have believed it of himself had anyone told him that this was the way hearing the news of almost having a child—especially so belatedly—would affect him.

But it was true. He, Ryan Colton, actually *wanted* children.

It was a hell of a thing to find out about himself at this stage of his life. Not only did he want children, but he wanted children *with Susie*.

Fat chance of that ever happening. You really messed that one up, the little voice in his head mocked.

Still, that one night they'd had together had brought back all the feelings he'd once had for her—rekindled all the old feelings and brought in a whole truckload of new ones.

And despite the tongue-lashing her mother had given him, Susie had not taken the opportunity to put him in his place or return to that state of polite avoidance that he and she had feigned during their last four years in the Tulsa police department.

Rather than go back to that behavior, Susie had

stepped up and let him know that she had his back in this ongoing investigation involving his family's ranch, as well as his sister.

Anyone else might have said that their one night together had been a slip and, more than that, a mistake. Moreover, they undoubtedly would have left him high and dry as far as any forensic and investigative backup might go.

But Susie hadn't.

Susie was there for him and *with* him. That had to mean something, didn't it?

Yeah, she was honorable, probably a lot more honorable than he would have been had the tables been reversed, he thought ruefully.

Ryan switched off the monitor and glared at the darkening computer screen. That mirrored, unfortunately, the state of the investigation right now, and possibly its continuing state in the foreseeable future.

For a second, Ryan chewed on the side of his lip, thinking.

Since Greta was at least out of jail, if not completely out of danger, and his mother was out of her coma and finally on the mend, maybe he could break off a tiny piece of time to get something resolved—between himself and Susie.

If he didn't do this now, it would only continue to bother him, only continue to grow until it became way too unmanageable.

Not that it would be any sort of a cakewalk for him

the way things stood right now, Ryan thought, revising his initial assessment of the situation before him.

This was no time for his courage to flag.

If he was going to do this, Ryan told himself, switching off his computer, he would do it right. There were steps to take, procedures to follow and things to prepare.

He felt the palms of his hands growing damp, which caught him by surprise. He was sweating. He, Ryan Colton, a former Marine, currently a detective with the Tulsa PD, who had found himself looking down the barrel of a gun more than once, talked down a killer in his day, all without breaking a sweat, he was perspiring like a high school freshman about to ask his first girl to the prom.

Hell, he hadn't even sweated it out then, he recalled. So why did what he was about to undertake make him feel so nervous now? He was a police detective, for God sakes.

Because if he did this, it would leave him completely exposed, completely vulnerable. Not even the bravest of men relished that kind of exposure.

But he was going to do this right. Because he had everything to win.

Or lose, that same nagging little voice whispered, not missing a single opportunity to gnaw away at his confidence.

Ryan stood in front of the somewhat weathered front door of the narrow two-story house, working up his courage to ring the doorbell. Considered tough and relentless by the people he went after, he found himself on the other side of an extremely rare, unsettling case of nerves. He'd faced down armed felons, not to mention the enemy, comprised of hostile, suicidal soldiers, on foreign soil halfway around the world. He'd done it without flinching.

Yet the thought of facing a petite older woman he literally towered over and outweighed by a third had him hesitating and rehearsing words in his head for what felt like the dozenth time.

He'd already made up his mind and knew he was going to ultimately go through with this whether or not Elizabeth Howard approved and gave her blessing, but he also knew it would go over so much more smoothly if he could get the woman to give him her stamp of approval.

Finally, because he was afraid that Mrs. Howard might suddenly choose to open the door and catch him at a disadvantage, Ryan forced himself to ring the doorbell. His fingertips felt cold and stiff, the way they might if he were the exposed, unwilling target of a sniper wearing night vision goggles at midnight.

The second he saw the front door opening, his heart rate sped up. And then all but stopped altogether.

It was now or never.

"Hello, Mrs. Howard."

Elizabeth Howard's soft, unlined face lost its natural smile and her expression hardened the instant that recognition set in. One hand remained on the door, holding it in place rather than opening it farther in an unspoken invitation.

There was no invitation in her eyes.

"I have nothing to say to you," she coldly told the man who she felt had broken her daughter's heart and ruined her life.

Ryan forced a smile to his lips. "That's all right, because I have something to say to you and I'd really like you to listen."

Elizabeth said nothing in response. The door remained just the way it was, as did she.

This was not going well, Ryan thought. A couple of years ago, he would have just turned on his heel and walked away. But then, a couple of years ago, he wouldn't have been here in the first place.

He was putting himself on the line, stripping himself bare and was, consequently, utterly vulnerable. But he had no choice. He'd come this far—he had to see this through. "May I come in, please? I'd rather not say this standing out here—and I don't think you'd want me to, either."

Still the woman said nothing, as if she was slowly turning over and examining not just each word, but each letter that went into making up each word. The silence dragged on, all but skewering itself into his chest.

Just when he was about to give up, Elizabeth took a small, measured step back, taking the door with her as she did.

"Make it quick."

He wasn't about to tell her that he couldn't "make it quick." That this was going to take a little time. But first things first. And first, he had to get inside the house.

Nodding at her, Ryan went in.

Susie had put in an extralong day at the lab, starting earlier than she normally did and remaining far later than was her custom. And she had done it all for a reason.

She'd gone through all the evidence with the proverbial fine-tooth comb, hoping that this time around, she would find a clue that she and the others had missed when they had initially gone over it.

There had to be something, she kept telling herself. There just had to be.

But so far, there wasn't.

Maybe she was just too tired to see it, she finally told herself just before she decided to call it a night and go home. She could always get an early start in the morning—but in order to do that, first she had to *leave* the office.

Putting one foot in front of the other, she did just that.

Dinner turned out to be some leftover something-

or-other she had no actual recollection of either buying or eating the first time around. Susie consumed it while standing over the sink, going over the case in her head one last time. When she was working on a case, everything else became secondary.

Everything but Ryan.

The annoying, accusing as well as unsettling thought seemed to just pop up in her head out of nowhere, as if to mock her and remind her that she was not an actual pillar of self-restraint and control.

Susie supposed that she could be forgiven that, seeing as she'd almost had a child with the man and, more than that, Ryan Colton was the only man she had ever really loved.

Oh, she'd been infatuated before, close to head over heels smitten before, but love? Actually in love? That had only happened to her once.

Yes, and then he dumped you, remember?

It wasn't exactly *dumping*, she silently argued. According to Ryan, his reasons for what he'd done had been complicated and he had broken up with her to keep them both safe, especially her.

Now, there was a new one, she couldn't help thinking. But because his excuse was so unique, she had to admit that it probably carried more than a germ of truth. Knowing Ryan the way she did, she could actually believe that *he* at least believed that was the reason he had done what he had.

She, however, couldn't come up with a scenario in

which breaking things off between them could even *remotely* be construed as being for her own good. "Good" to her revolved around having Ryan in her world. Having him love her, having him want her.

Having him—

Having *him*, she thought, smiling to herself as her imagination began to take off.

Knock it off, Howard, she upbraided herself sternly. *Stop building a case for something that isn't there, that isn't going to happen. You enjoyed some really good sex, but it didn't come with strings or any terms for renewal. It was hot and it was brief. Get used to it.*

And then get over it.

She was so involved in her thoughts, she almost didn't hear the doorbell. The more emphatic knocking, however, did register.

Feeling a little leery now that she knew there was someone out there attacking people within Ryan's sphere of friends and family, Susie took her handgun with her to the door. Just to be on the safe side.

"Who is it?" she asked, standing a good three feet away from the door. She'd stepped over Conway to get this close. The dog was sleeping and apparently the knocking had done nothing to change the border collie's state.

"Good, you're finally asking that before you open the door," he said with approval.

"Ryan?"

"None other," he confirmed.

Surprised and trying not to notice the way her heart suddenly decided to accelerate, Susie quickly unlocked the door.

"I see you were expecting me," he deadpanned. In this case, he felt that humor was his best defense.

The first thing he noticed when she opened the door to admit him was the way Susie's cheeks were flushed. They did that whenever she was surprised.

The second thing he noticed was the gun in her hand. Her finger was still poised on the trigger, but the muzzle was pointed down.

Her eyebrows drew together in confusion. "What?" When he nodded at the handgun in response to her question, she put it down.

"What happened to your 'security system'?" he asked.

"Conway's had a long day," she said in the dog's defense. The pet's faint snoring could be heard. "What are you doing here?" she asked, closing the door behind him.

He decided to gauge the atmosphere and approach his subject slowly. "I wanted to talk to you."

They'd interacted off and on all day. She'd thought he was as worn-out at the edges as she was. Had he come up with a new angle on his way home?

"About the case?" she asked.

"Yes." It was the first word on his lips, but he didn't want to start off by lying, so he said, "No, not really." Pausing for a moment, more for courage than for dramatic effect, he began, "I wanted to talk about us."

"Us?" she echoed uncertainly.

Ryan looked at her. He couldn't approach this by pussyfooting around the subject, so he dove straight into the deep end. "Why didn't you tell me that you were pregnant?"

Susie blew out a breath, the kind one exhaled when they were punched in the gut. That was how she felt, dealing with this question and its answer.

"Because I didn't want you 'doing the right thing' just because I was carrying your baby," she told him honestly. "If you were going to ask to marry me, I wanted it to be because you were in love with me, not because your family expected you to own up to your responsibilities by marrying the girl you accidentally got pregnant. And, anyway, one way or the other," she added with a careless shrug, "you're off the hook now."

"I don't consider the thought of marrying you as being 'on the hook,'" he told her, clarifying how he felt—or at least thinking that he was.

She shrugged as if the whole thing didn't matter to her one way or another. She'd worked hard to be able to summon this facade of disinterest at will. But even so, it was a struggle for her. "Either way, you're free."

His eyes met hers. "Is that what you really think?" he asked.

She hesitated at first, then fell back on the careless shrug. "Well, yes."

Ryan laughed softly to himself. "Then maybe you're not as smart as I thought you were." Enough with the bandying things back and forth. Time to get down to the heart of why he was here. "I want to marry you, Susie."

The words stunned her for a second, but then she managed to collect herself. It was just talk, nothing more, Susie told herself.

"Why, because you're a Colton and you've got a code to uphold?" she challenged.

Ryan took hold of her shoulders, bracketing her in place. "No, because I'm in love with you and I don't want to face the next forty to fifty years without you right there by my side. I want you *with* me."

Susie's mouth went dry. *Words, just words. He knows how to use them, how to get your defenses down.* "You don't know what you're saying," she told him, dismissing what he had just told her.

The laugh was a dry one. "Funny, that's what your mother said earlier when I went to talk to her."

That caught her completely off guard. "You went to talk to my mother?" Her mother had made it clear in no uncertain terms that she couldn't stand the sight of him. Why in heaven's name had he gone over to her mother's house?

Ryan nodded in response to her question. "Yes."

She had to ask. "Why?"

"To ask for permission to marry you."

To hell with a dry mouth—it fell completely open this time. "What did she say?" As if she didn't know, Susie thought.

"Well, at first I think she wanted to have me drawn and quartered, and it took some doing, but I finally convinced your mother that I was serious. I told her that ever since I found out about the baby you lost, I couldn't stop thinking about it. I told her that I wanted another chance to have a baby with you. Lots of babies."

Her eyes widened, just like her mouth had. Disbelief and amazement highlighted her face. "And she believed you?"

"Not at first," Ryan qualified. "But I can be very persuasive when I want to be—and I really wanted to be," he added.

She still didn't know whether or not to believe him. It would require ignoring her fear of getting irrevocably hit emotionally. "And you're serious?"

"Never more serious in my whole life," he swore, crossing his heart like a small child might do. He was leaving no base uncovered. "I've made some mistakes in my life, but not a day goes by that I don't regret ending it between us. I didn't fully realize just how much you lit up my world until you weren't there to do it anymore."

Her mind was desperately scrambling to understand and absorb what she was hearing. After first wanting him, then wanting to get over him, she needed to get every single word straight.

"So what you're saying is—"

He answered her in quick succession. "I want to marry you. I want to have children with you. I want to have grandchildren with you and I want to grow old with you—"

"Ryan?" She finally managed to get him to pause long enough to hear her.

He looked at her, afraid of what he might hear, his mind searching for a way to convince her to say yes.

"What?"

"Are you planning on shutting up anytime soon?" she asked him.

Thrown off by her question, Ryan cocked his head, curious. "Why?"

"Because I'd like to kiss you and it's very hard to kiss a moving target," she told him.

"I can shut up," he said in all seriousness.

"Good. Then do it," she told him, throwing her arms around his neck.

He had enough time to enfold her in his arms and bring her closer to him. "Then you'll marry me?"

Her answer was yes. It had always been yes. But for now, she was enjoying the moment and played it out a little longer.

"We'll talk," she promised. "Later."

The last word fluttered across his mouth a microsecond before her mouth met his.

Conway raised his head as if to check them out, yipped his approval once, then went back to sleep.

Susie and Ryan were otherwise occupied. They didn't talk for a long, long time.

Epilogue

Restless, the tall, willowy-figured young woman paced about the small hotel room like a caged animal longing for freedom.

Freedom, *her* freedom, was coming.

But it wasn't coming soon enough.

Alice could feel the impatience clawing at her throat. She was desperate to implement the last part of her detailed plan.

She was through with playing games, Alice thought with a surge of anticipated triumph. Through with poking a stick at her prey, watching her squirm from a distance. Her strikes had been getting closer and closer to the center of Greta's world, but the excitement of those strikes wasn't enough anymore.

Weren't enough to keep her anger contained.

Not anymore.

She was tired of being patient, tired of waiting on the sidelines, tired of a life of deprivation and living on crumbs while that bitch with her face got to live like a queen.

It wasn't fair!

Why had that man picked her sister and not her? She'd seen that photograph, the only one that existed of the two of them. There hadn't been an iota of difference between them. They'd been babies, not even a week old at the time.

Like two damn peas in a stupid pod.

What had set the two of them apart for him?

Why her and not me? her mind demanded for the hundredth time.

The question echoed over and over again in Alice's head, growing louder. It was so loud it was almost deafening.

Or maybe the question was actually echoing around the room.

Was that her voice she heard?

Abruptly, she stopped pacing in front of the stained dresser. Alice stared at her reflection in the mirror that hung just above it.

They hadn't looked any different then and they didn't look any different now.

Well, maybe she was a little prettier, Alice decided,

looking at herself, but not to the point that it could set them apart if they weren't standing side by side.

She had diligently done her homework once she'd found out that she had a twin. A drunken confession from her piece of trash of a mother had opened her eyes to the injustice that had occurred in her life before she ever had any recollection of it. Slurring her words, her mother had actually had the gall to look at her and complain that maybe she'd sold the wrong twin. Maybe she should have kept the other one and sold her because the other one had turned out to be a better daughter.

She'd had to threaten her mother with a broken whiskey bottle to get the rest of the story out of her. But once she'd heard it, she knew what she had to do.

It was all as clear as crystal mountain water to her. She had to find that bitch, find some way to get rid of her.

But first she was going to make her pay. Pay for the miserable life she'd had to endure while her worthless twin got to play the adored little rich girl, even getting her picture in the paper just because she was going to be marrying the brother of some big-time CEO or something like that.

It should have been her.

It was *going* to be her.

All she had to do was kill Greta and take her place. No big deal.

* * * * *

If you loved this romantic, no-thrills-barred story,
don't miss these books from Marie Ferrarella:

HOW TO SEDUCE A CAVANAUGH
CAVANAUGH FORTUNE
CAVANAUGH STRONG
CAVANAUGH UNDERCOVER

Also, don't miss the next book in
THE COLTONS OF OKLAHOMA *series,*
THE COLTON BODYGUARD by Carla Cassidy,
available November 2015 from
Harlequin Romantic Suspense.

For a sneak peek, turn the page!

Chapter 1

*T*he jail cell door clanked shut behind Greta Colton. She turned and grabbed the bars, staring at her brother on the other side.

"Ryan, you know this is all a mistake. I didn't kill anyone. I'm innocent. I didn't kill Kurt." She watched in horror as Ryan turned his back on her and walked away. How could he believe she was capable of murder?

"Ryan, please." She grasped the cell bars more tightly, frantic for him, for anyone to believe her. "I'm not a murderer," she screamed, but he didn't stop walking away from her.

Greta sat up and looked around, disoriented as to the time and place. Her pounding heart slowed.

She was safe in her king-size bed in her bedroom. A glance at the clock on the nightstand indicated it was just after four in the afternoon.

She was safe beneath her sky-blue comforter with the afternoon sunshine drifting through the lacy white curtains at the window. She released a sigh of relief.

The nightmare she'd just suffered had become a familiar one over the past three weeks, when she really had been arrested for the murder of ranch hand Kurt Rodgers.

She'd decided to take a short nap after lunch, but had slept longer than she had intended. Lately sleeping had been far easier than being fully conscious and in the present.

The moments before and since she'd been released from jail had been fraught with anger, sadness, lies and questions. It wasn't just her who had been through hell, but her family, as well.

She got out of bed and walked to the nearby window. From this vantage point she could see much of the green pastures and impressive outbuildings of the family ranch, the Lucky C.

But ranch business was the last thing on her mind. A lie had gotten her out of jail, ruined her engagement and destroyed her mother's happiness in planning a wedding. For the past two and a half weeks Greta had been living like a hermit, trying to cope with everything that had happened to forever change her life.

She left the window and headed for the shower in the luxurious bathroom just off the sitting area in her bedroom. It was time for her to face the man who had lied for her, the man who had sworn that on the night of Kurt's murder he was in a hotel room with her in Oklahoma City.

She *had* been in a hotel room in Oklahoma City, but she'd been all alone, certainly not with Tyler Stanton, her future brother-in-law. She definitely hadn't been carrying on a torrid affair with Tyler as he had implied to the police when he'd offered up the alibi that had ultimately released her from jail.

It didn't take her long to shower and dress in a pair of tailored brown slacks and a russet blouse that she knew complimented her slender figure. She pulled on a pair of brown suede dress boots and slipped inside her right boot the knife her father had given her when she'd turned sixteen years old.

Her father had worried about her having the run of the ranch, dealing with ranch hands who appeared to be good guys but might be a danger to her, so he'd gifted her with the knife for self-protection. He'd also told her not to pull it on somebody unless she had the guts to use it.

When closed it was a beautiful palm-size mother-of-pearl case, but with a click of a button it became a wicked, nearly five-inch-length weapon. Thankfully she had never had to use it or even take it out of her boot.

She left the Lucky C by one of the back doors, grateful when she didn't encounter anyone. She didn't want anyone knowing where she was going. Thankfully the only person in the family who knew she'd been alibied with the lie of an affair was her brother, Ryan, and a couple of the officers who worked for the Tulsa police force. As far as she knew none of them had shared that information with anyone else.

So far she'd been spared the humiliating experience of trying to explain to her parents and siblings that she wasn't having an affair, no matter what Tyler had told the authorities.

It was almost seven when she pulled her red Jeep just inside the black wrought-iron gates at the entrance to Tyler Stanton's estate. It was an hour-and-a-half drive from the Colton ranch in Tulsa to Tyler's home in Oklahoma City.

Throughout the drive several times she'd considered turning around and heading back to the ranch. But ultimately she knew she had to confront Tyler and tonight was as good a time as any. She hadn't spoken to or seen him since being released from jail. She needed answers that only he could give her.

She stopped the Jeep when the impressive sprawling ranch house came into view. It was definitely the living space of a successful man and Tyler was definitely successful. As owner and CEO of Stanton Oil, he was ridiculously handsome and socially sought after for various fund-raisers and events. The few times Greta had been around him she'd always found him slightly cold and very intimidating.

Why would he risk his good reputation and his relationship with his brother, Mark, by implicating himself in an affair with her?

Thankfully he must've greased some palms to keep her alibi quiet for there had been no hint of tawdry rumors floating around. Of course, Mark had heard and had ridden into the Colton house a week ago on a self-righteous horse and declared their engagement over.

She'd spent five days in jail and for the past week she'd been on the phone canceling wedding arrangements that had been made and praying her mother didn't spiral down into one of the deep depressions that had often occurred through most of Greta's life.

Stalling, she now thought. She was stalling by sitting here and staring at Tyler's house. She put the Jeep into Drive and moved forward, swallowing against the swell of anxiety that tried to waltz up the back of her throat.

She didn't have the answers to a lot of things that had been happening at the Colton ranch but she could at least get an answer from Tyler as to why he had lied for her.

She parked right in front of the house. Light spilled from several windows, breaking through the falling darkness of the early-November night.

Tyler had a reputation as a workaholic. It was possible he wasn't even home yet. If he wasn't, then she'd wait. If his household help didn't want her inside then she'd wait in her vehicle. She'd already put this conversation off for far too long.

Getting out of her car she fought against the nervous energy that sizzled through her. She had nothing to be anxious about—after all, he was the one who had told the outrageous lie. But Tyler had always made her nervous with his cold blue eyes and hint of disdain when he looked at her.

She straightened her shoulders resolutely and rang the bell, hearing the musical chimes respond from someplace inside. As she waited she pulled up the collar of her lightweight beige coat against the chilly evening air.

The door opened and she wasn't sure who was more surprised, herself or Tyler. She'd expected a housekeeper, but instead a Tyler Stanton she'd never seen before stood in front of her.

The few times they had ever had any interaction Tyler had always been impeccably dressed. The Tyler before her was absent his suit coat and tie. His white shirt was half-unbuttoned to reveal just enough bare chest to be distracting and his short light brown hair was slightly mussed. His dark blue eyes appeared to take in the whole sum of her with a quick sweep from head to toe.

"Greta, I was wondering when or if I'd ever hear

from you. Please come in." He opened the door wider to allow her into a large foyer. "May I take your coat?"

Before she could reply he had removed her coat and hung it in the nearby closet. He then smoothly ushered her into the great room and offered her a seat on a plush black leather sofa.

It was as if she'd entered an alternate universe. The Tyler she knew was stiff and formal, but this Tyler appeared casual and surprisingly welcoming. "How about something to drink? Maybe a glass of wine?" he asked.

"That would be nice." She finally found her voice.

"Red or white?" He moved to an elaborate built-in bar on one side of the large room.

"White would be fine," she replied.

"How have you been?" he asked and strode across the expanse of the room to hand her a crystal long-stemmed glass of wine.

He sat next to her and set his own glass of wine on the glass-topped coffee table in front of them.

"I've been better," she replied. He sat so close to her she could smell the scent of his spicy cologne, so different than Mark's woodsy favorite scent. "I guess you heard that Mark broke off our engagement."

His gaze held hers intently. "Are you heartbroken over it?"

She hesitated, wondering if she should lie and make Tyler feel bad. "No, I'm only sorry he beat me to the punch," she replied honestly. "I was behind bars for five long days and nights and he didn't even visit me once. Five days in jail gave me a lot of time to think. In fact I've heard from a couple of my friends that while I was locked up Mark was making the rounds, visiting his old girlfriends, so I'd intended to break things off with him anyway. But that's not why I'm here."

She paused and took a sip of her wine and then set the glass down. She eyed the handsome man beside her boldly. "Why, Tyler? Why did you lie for me?"

"Because I knew you were no murderer," he replied easily.

"Didn't you hear that my DNA and fingerprints were all over the crime scene? My own brother arrested me." Pain swept through her as she remembered Ryan placing handcuffs on her and putting her into the back of his patrol car.

"I also know they had a hotel receipt to support the fact that you checked into the Regent Hotel on the night that Kurt was murdered, but since you were alone and had no further interaction with the hotel staff nobody could substantiate your alibi for later in the evening. Besides, I didn't care what incriminating evidence they had. I knew you didn't have it in you to hurt anyone. I lied because you needed an alibi and I knew nobody would question my word."

There was no arrogance in his tone—it was just a statement of fact that reminded her that Tyler was an important, powerful businessman, not just in Oklahoma City but in Tulsa, as well.

"Why on earth would you even involve yourself with my problems?" She knew that he and Mark weren't particularly close, so she couldn't believe he'd intervened for Mark's sake, especially given the alibi he provided—being her lover.

Her cheeks warmed at the thought. She had a feeling when Tyler Stanton made love to a woman it would be more like a total body-and-soul possession rather than just a pleasant sexual encounter.

Tyler leaned toward her, his nearness seeming to suck all of the oxygen out of the air. His blue eyes were piercing, as if wanting to see something deep inside her. "Do you really want to know why I got you out of jail? Why I involved myself in your life?"

She nodded. She'd never noticed before how easy it would be to fall into the depths of his dark blue eyes and how hypnotic his smooth, deep voice could be. She leaned toward him, as if anticipating a secret that might change her life and right her world forever.

"Mark was never supposed to take you for himself. That day in April I sent him to meet with you because I had a troubled horse that I wanted your help with. But I also wanted to get you here and hopefully into my bed."

She reeled back, shocked by his words. "What are you talking about? Mark never mentioned a horse to me that first day he came to the ranch to see me."

She didn't even want to address the rest of what he'd said to her. She could scarcely wrap her brain around his bold audacity.

"No, I'm sure he didn't," Tyler replied drily. "He simply set out to win your heart for himself and he accomplished that."

He picked up his wineglass, took a sip and then set the glass back down. "Despite my own desire for you, I was happy for Mark when the two of you got engaged in June. My brother and I see eye to eye on few things, but I wanted him to be happy, and if you were his happiness then I would have never done or said anything to ruin things for the two of you."

"Mark is happiest when he's the center of attention," she replied drily. "But he only wants positive attention. I always suspected that when I was at home on the ranch in Tulsa and he was at his town house here in Oklahoma City, he was seeing other women."

Tyler said nothing, but in his silence Greta recognized the truth. Mark had never really loved her. He had been in love with marrying a Colton, with all the society-page tidbits about their romance and upcoming wedding. But he'd never truly loved Greta, the tomboy who was happiest wearing jeans and a sweatshirt and working with and training horses.

"I thought that the relationship with you might make a man out of him," he said. "But I guess I was wrong."

"Do you still have that troubled horse?" she asked, eager to turn the course of the conversation.

"I do. She's a three-year-old filly who has had no training and very little human contact. Are you interested in working with her?"

"I might be," she replied. She needed something to focus on besides the fact that the man she'd nearly married wasn't in love with her and she really hadn't loved him. She needed a challenge to take her mind off all the strange and frightening things that had been happening in her life and around the Colton ranch.

"I still have the horse and I still have an intense desire for you. Would you also be interested in sharing my bed tonight?" he asked.

Tyler wasn't a man who believed in playing games. He believed in going after what he wanted, and he had wanted Greta Colton since the very first time he'd seen her.

It was obvious he'd shocked her with his indecent and unexpected proposal to share his bed. She grabbed her wineglass and downed the contents, her cheeks a becoming pink.

Although she looked lovely now in the tailored slacks that hugged her long legs and the rust-colored blouse that enhanced her hazel-green eyes and her dark brown hair, she had really caught his attention when he'd watched her working with a horse at a rodeo months earlier.

Then, her slender figure had been clad in dusty

jeans and a T-shirt, and she'd commanded the horse with confidence and mastery. That had been the woman who had both captured his desire and intrigued him.

She lowered her glass and tucked a strand of her long wavy hair behind her ear. "You're something else," she finally said. "You make up an outrageous lie to get me out of jail, a lie that ruined my engagement, and now you have the audacity to ask me to sleep with you?"

He smiled. "Sleep wasn't exactly what I had in mind." Her cheeks flushed with color once again, but she made no move to leave. "Greta, we're both consenting adults and don't need to answer to anyone for what we do," he added.

"I don't just fall into bed with any man who asks me," she replied and straightened her back defensively.

"I'm aware of that," he said. "If you were that kind of woman then I wouldn't be interested in you."

She stared at him and then looked away. "Could I please have another glass of wine?" she asked. "And let's talk a bit more about this horse you have."

He got up and refilled her glass, then sat down again, this time a little bit closer to her…close enough that he could smell the fresh scent of her.

It was crazy, he had never felt such a visceral pull toward a woman before or since that first time he'd seen Greta. He'd initially been disappointed when he realized Mark and Greta had become an item, but he'd also been pleased that his younger brother had found somebody and intended to settle down.

It didn't take long for Tyler to realize that Mark had no intention of settling down, wedding or not. Getting engaged and planning a wedding to Greta hadn't slowed Mark's womanizing ways or forced him to begin to build a future of financial stability for himself and his wife.

"What else do you want to know about the horse?" he asked.

Her gaze danced down to his exposed chest and then quickly moved back up to his face. "Uh…how did you come to own her?"

That quick glance emboldened him. She apparently wasn't completely immune to him. "I was driving to work one day and passed a field where the horse was tethered to a post. She was half-starved and appeared to have been whipped. I couldn't just drive by and forget about her obvious distress, so I stopped at the closest ranch house and the man living there told me the horse was his. I offered to buy her and after some negotiation, he agreed. Since then she's filled out and healed from her physical abuse, but neither of my ranch hands have been able to work with her. She won't let anyone near her."

"It sounds like you probably saved her life," Greta replied, more than a hint of approval in her voice.

"If I did, she isn't showing any gratitude," he replied drily. He was rewarded by her short but melodic laugh. "And speaking of gratitude, I haven't heard you thank me for getting you out of jail."

"I am grateful, but I'm not sure I've forgiven you for the particular lie you told. Didn't you consider what it might do to my reputation? What it would do to your relationship with your brother? Didn't you consider any of the consequences of your lie?"

"Nothing has gone public, so your good reputation remains intact." He paused and thought about his brother. "Mark and I have always had a difficult relationship. To be honest, I knew that you'd already told the authorities that you were in a hotel room on the night of the murder. It just seemed easiest for me to tell them that I was in that room with you. I wasn't thinking of consequences, I just couldn't stand the thought of you having to spend another day and another night in that jail cell."

She sighed and took a drink from her glass. "It would have been so much easier if Mark had been the one to come forward and say he was with me that night." Her eyes narrowed. "But he did absolutely nothing to help me. He didn't even come to see me or make a phone call to check on me."

"If all this hadn't happened then you wouldn't have known that you were about to marry the wrong man," Tyler countered. "Not that I'm suggesting I'm the right man."

She tilted her head slightly and looked at him curiously. "Why haven't you married? You're handsome and successful and I'm sure plenty of women would be happy to become Mrs. Tyler Stanton."

"The women who want to be my wife aren't the kind of women I'd want for a wife. They want it for all the wrong reasons," he replied. "I got close to marrying once, but it didn't work out, and since then I haven't found the right woman. Besides, I work long hours and don't have a lot of time to do the whole dating thing."

"So, you just invite emotionally vulnerable women to share your bed for the night and then move on to the next woman." She stared at him boldly.

A small laugh escaped him. "You don't appear to me to be an emotionally vulnerable woman and no, I don't make a habit of inviting women into my bed. In fact, you're the first who has gotten an official invitation."

She eyed him dubiously.

He leaned closer to her, so close that if he wanted to he could wrap her in his arms and take full possession of her lush lips with his. It was tempting. It was oh, so tempting.

"It's true, Greta," he said and watched her eyes spark with gold and green hues. "I don't invite women into my bed. I wait for them to invite me into theirs. But you're different and the desire, the passion I have for you, is stronger than anything I've ever felt for any other woman."

Her mouth trembled slightly and he continued, "In all my life I've never been jealous of Mark, but when he hooked up with you, I was jealous of him for the first time. He had what I wanted…what I still want."

"I should go," she replied in a breathy voice, but she made no move to get up.

"You should stay," he countered. "It's a long drive back to Tulsa. You should stay here with me tonight and then tomorrow morning you can see the horse."

Her eyes looked slightly glazed and he didn't know if it was from the wine she'd drank too fast or the blatant lust he knew shone from his own.

"Greta, if you want, you can spend the night in one of my guest rooms." It wasn't what he wanted, but he also didn't want to coerce her in any way. He'd laid his cards out on the table and the next play was hers.

"I'll stay," she said slowly. "I'll stay in one of your guest rooms and take a look at the horse in the morning and decide if she's a project I want to take on."

Disappointment winged through him, but he tamped it down. He knew he'd been forward and he really wasn't surprised by her answer. He'd definitely been too open too quickly. It had been out of character for him, but when he'd seen her standing on his front porch all of his desire for her that had simmered for so long had roared to full life.

"Then whenever you're ready I'll show you to your room," he replied.

"I think I'm ready now." She stood and finished the last drink of wine in her glass.

He got up as well, took the glass from her and carried it and his own to the bar. He felt her gaze on his back and cursed himself for being a fool.

He should have just told her he'd alibied her because he'd been sure of her innocence and then told her about the horse he wanted her to work with. He should have never come at her with the open and honest passion that had been in his heart and beat through his veins.

"I'll get you a T-shirt to sleep in," he said as he led her down the long hallway. They passed several bedrooms and two baths before he finally turned into a room that was located next to his master suite.

"This is lovely," she said. She offered him a small smile. "My bedroom at home is decorated in shades of blue, too."

"Then you should feel right at home here. There's an en suite bathroom where you should find whatever you need. There's several new toothbrushes beneath the sink and if you need something else that you can't find, just ask."

"I'm sure I'll be fine," she replied.

"I'll just go grab a T-shirt for you to sleep in."

He left her standing in the guest room and went into his master suite, to the drawer that held his T-shirts. He pulled one out and for a brief moment imagined her wearing it and nothing else.

He shook his head and shoved the vision aside, and then returned to the guest room, where she hadn't moved a foot.

He handed her the T-shirt. "Thanks, this should be more comfortable than trying to sleep in my clothes," she said. She shifted from one booted foot to the other, obviously uncomfortable.

"Then I'll just tell you good-night," he said. "I'm right next door if you can't find what you need or if you change your mind about joining me." Damn, he'd done it again.

"You're very persistent," she replied.

"I am when I know what I want."

"Good night, Tyler," she said.

"Good night." He left the room and she closed the door behind him. He headed back to the great room and to the bar to put the glasses they had used into the dishwasher in the kitchen.

He certainly didn't intend to give up on satisfying his desire for Greta. He'd shocked her tonight, but he could be a patient man and he'd swear there had been more than a hint of interest in her eyes.

Tonight wasn't the end of things with Greta. He had a feeling it was just the beginning. All he had to do was convince her of that fact.

ROMANTIC suspense

Available November 3, 2015

#1871 THE COLTON BODYGUARD

The Coltons of Oklahoma • by Carla Cassidy

When Greta Colton is wrongfully arrested for murder, Tyler Stanton unhesitatingly provides an alibi—she was in his arms all night! But more than false accusations endanger the beautiful horse trainer...and Tyler might be the only one who can save her from the oncoming danger.

#1872 COWBOY CHRISTMAS RESCUE

by Beth Cornelison and Colleen Thompson

When shots interrupt a Christmas ranch wedding, two couples must track down a wannabe killer to stay alive. Former bull rider Nate Wheeler protects his wife-to-be, who's carrying the most precious gift of all—their child. At the same time, sheriff Brady McCall puts his life on the line for his former love, who witnessed the crime.

#1873 HER CHRISTMAS PROTECTOR

Silver Valley P.D. • by Geri Krotow

Undercover for a government shadow agency, Zora Krasny has to keep her eye on the prize: bringing down a serial killer. But she's distracted when she teams up with her childhood crush, Detective Bryce Campbell, who looks oh-so-good while bringing down bad guys. Can Zora and Bryce catch a criminal *and* write their own happily-ever-after?

#1874 KILLER SEASON • by Lara Lacombe

When grad student Fiona Sanders is rescued from a gunpoint robbery, she can't help but feel gratitude—and maybe a little more—for handsome cop Nate Gallagher. But before the two can explore their attraction, Fiona becomes a criminal's target! It's up to this Texas twosome to solve the crime—and find the keys to each others' hearts.

SPECIAL EXCERPT FROM

H HARLEQUIN®

ROMANTIC suspense

*When horse trainer Greta Colton is wrongfully
imprisoned, oilman Tyler Stanton gives her an alibi—and
provides protection. But Tyler aims to safeguard more
than Greta's body. He'll also have to lasso her heart...*

*Read on for a sneak preview of
THE COLTON BODYGUARD,
the thrilling conclusion to the 2015
COLTONS OF OKLAHOMA continuity.*

"If all this hadn't happened, then you wouldn't have known
that you were about to marry the wrong man," Tyler countered. "Not that I'm suggesting I'm the right man."

She tilted her head slightly and looked at him
curiously. "Why haven't you married? You're handsome
and successful and I'm sure plenty of women would be
happy to become Mrs. Tyler Stanton."

"The women who want to be my wife aren't the kind
of woman I'd want for a wife. They want it for all the
wrong reasons," he replied. "I got close to marrying once,
but it didn't work out and since then I haven't found the
right woman. Besides, I work long hours and don't have
a lot of time to do the whole dating thing."

"So you just invite emotionally vulnerable women to
share your bed for the night and then move on to the next
woman." She stared at him boldly.

A small laugh escaped him. "You don't appear to me
to be an emotionally vulnerable woman and no, I don't

make a habit of inviting women into my bed. In fact, you're the first who has gotten an official invitation."

She eyed him dubiously.

He leaned closer to her, so close that if he wanted to, he could wrap her in his arms and take full possession of her lush lips with his. It was tempting. It was oh so tempting.

"It's true, Greta," he said and watched her eyes spark with gold and green hues. "I don't invite women into my bed. I wait for them to invite me into theirs. But you're different and the desire, the passion, I have for you is stronger than anything I've ever felt for any other woman."

Her mouth trembled slightly and he continued, "In all of my life I've never been jealous of Mark, but when he hooked up with you, I was jealous of him for the first time. He had what I wanted…what I still want."

Don't miss
THE COLTON BODYGUARD
by New York Times *bestselling author Carla Cassidy,*
available November 2015 wherever
Harlequin® Romantic Suspense
books and ebooks are sold.

www.Harlequin.com

Turn your love of reading into rewards you'll love with
Harlequin My Rewards

THE WORLD IS BETTER WITH

Romance

Harlequin has everything from contemporary, passionate and heartwarming to suspenseful and inspirational stories.

Whatever your mood,
we have a romance just for you!

Connect with us to find your next great read,
special offers and more.

f /HarlequinBooks

🐦 @HarlequinBooks

www.HarlequinBlog.com

www.Harlequin.com/Newsletters

⬧ HARLEQUIN®

A *Romance* FOR EVERY MOOD™

www.Harlequin.com